"It's you
"What games shall we play?"

Corey shivered. She'd never played games, not the kind he meant. "Well," she said nervously, "you could be Tarzan and I could be Jane. Or you could be Robin Hood and I'll—"

"Or I could be Nick and you could be Corey and we could just let nature take its course." Slowly, holding her gaze, he unbuttoned his khaki pants and pulled the zipper down.

Feeling her cheeks flame, she said, "Couldn't I just close my eyes and let you surprise me?"

He grinned. "As I said before, it's your party. You want a surprise, I'll give you a surprise."

She closed her eyes. In the velvety blackness, she heard the rustle of fabric hitting the floor, a soft footstep. In her mind's eye, she could see him in all his naked glory. And then hands on her waist lifted her, peeled away her clothes…

She stood there, eyes pressed shut, feeling dizzy and disoriented and sexier than she'd ever felt in her life. "Now what?" she murmured.

"Whatever you like," he replied.

Dear Reader,

Interested in the exciting life of a real private eye?
You've come to the right place! Years ago, I had a chance
to fill in at a detective agency. "Oh, boy," thought I, then
a budding romance novelist, "I'll get lots of exciting
ideas for books!"

What I got was tired hands from all that typing. Most of
the reports went something like this: "Subject entered
house at 8:07 p.m. Subject reappeared at 7:53 a.m."
Blah, blah and so forth; I yawned a *lot.*

But now that I think about it, one of the detectives was
kind of cute. And he did spring to mind occasionally
while I was writing *A Private Eyeful,* so perhaps my stint
as a "Girl Friday" really was time well spent. Of course,
the most important thing is that *you* think so after you
read the results!

I hope you've enjoyed *all* the wonderful books in the
Hero for Hire miniseries.

Ruth Jean Dale

Books by Ruth Jean Dale

HARLEQUIN TEMPTATION

A PRIVATE EYEFUL
Ruth Jean Dale

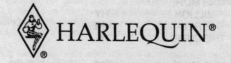

HARLEQUIN®

TORONTO • NEW YORK • LONDON
AMSTERDAM • PARIS • SYDNEY • HAMBURG
STOCKHOLM • ATHENS • TOKYO • MILAN • MADRID
PRAGUE • WARSAW • BUDAPEST • AUCKLAND

For Susan Sheppard, who "discovered" me—not at a soda fountain in Hollywood, but in a pizza parlor in San Diego. Little did we know…!

ISBN 0-373-25809-7

A PRIVATE EYEFUL

Copyright © 1998 by Betty Duran.

Prologue

THE SEXY CADENCE of a woman's spike heels on hard wooden floors sent an expectant shiver through the waiting man. The rhythmic sound ceased abruptly just beyond the closed office door, to be replaced by an indistinct murmur of voices.

Ignoring a slight tensing of his shoulders, Nicholas Charles continued to stare out the third-floor window at a fabulous view of the Golden Gate Bridge and San Francisco Bay. He knew what that sound meant: Samantha Joan Spade had arrived. After nearly four years in the employ of the S. J. Spade Insurance Agency— insurance in quotes— he was about to come face-to-face with his boss for the very first time.

To call her insistence on keeping a low profile eccentric would be an understatement. Although he'd spoken to her a few times on the telephone, he'd routinely been handed his assignments by her office staff, without ever encountering the boss lady herself.

All that was now about to change. Keeping his breathing light and steady, he told himself he was ready for anything. He hoped it was true, but he had a funny feeling it might not be.

The truth was, Nick knew almost nothing about the mysterious S. J. Spade beyond the obvious: that her insurance agency was really a front to guard the privacy of her personal-protection clientele. Casual pumping and prying of her office staff had netted him the barest facts: that she'd inherited the agency from a deceased husband who'd been a private detective, that she had no children, no pets, no known vices or addictions that anyone knew of, and that she was damn good at providing peerless personal protection, for a price.

After a while, Nick had stopped asking. Then he got "The Call."

The Call came less than an hour after he'd safely delivered the wife of an international industrialist to a secret location in London, where her grateful husband waited anxiously. Nick had provided "insurance" for the terrified middle-aged woman, which included snatching her from beneath the noses of a gang of kidnappers, then hiding out with her in a cabin in the Adirondacks until the time was right for a white-knuckle dash to Kennedy Airport and an equally nerve-racking flight across the Atlantic.

It had been his third assignment in a row without more than a couple of days off in between. He figured he'd earned a nice, long vacation, and he'd been all set to take it—until the telephone in his hotel room rang mere minutes after he walked in.

After the obligatory congratulations-on-a-job-well-done, Mark Spenser, Ms. Spade's San Francisco liaison, had announced, "She wants to see you."

"You mean in person?"

"That's right."

Nick felt a spark of interest that quickly died. He was too damn tired to care much. "When?"

"Yesterday." Mark sounded cheerful, as if he was enjoying this a shade too much. "I've already booked your flight out of Heathrow. You leave at five-fifteen."

"Not a chance. I couldn't get to the airport in time, even if I left now."

"Not to worry. Ms. Spade has friends in unexpected places. We've arranged an escort—"

"But until an hour ago, you didn't even know this job was finished."

"—should be arriving just about—"

There was a firm knock on the hotel door. A London bobby stood there, smiling and polite. Nick surrendered himself into the hands of the British law without the faintest idea how the rendezvous had been accomplished.

Now safely ensconsed in the boss's office with a bad case of jet lag compounded by mental exhaustion, he struggled to keep focused. In a battle of wits, he knew he was only half-armed at this moment. He also knew instinctively that it would take everything he had to deal with the hitherto elusive Samantha Spade.

And on her turf, yet—her private office on the third floor of the agency's headquarters in a Queen Anne row house on one of San Francisco's many hills. He'd been surprised when Charilyn, the office manager, had opened the boss lady's door and invited him inside to wait. He'd given her a startled glance; she'd raised her brows and shrugged.

"*She's* not worried," Charilyn said with a grin. "What'cha gonna do, rifle through the files?"

Laughing, she'd closed the door behind her, leaving him alone.

And Nick had rifled through the files. He couldn't help it. It was his nature, his training and his profession to spot danger before it spotted him or those he'd been hired to protect. The agency's motto—Call 1-800-HERO—was more than a gimmick to him.

The files were mostly archives of old, cleared cases. No personal notes, a few personal photos of men he didn't recognize, nothing much to reveal the personality of the woman who worked here beyond the fact that she apparently enjoyed the opposite sex. All he found that seemed out of place was a blotter covered with doodles of a single word: *Laura*.

Mildly interesting, but hardly dangerous.

Too whipped to act the professional snoop any longer, he'd decided to enjoy the view and let Samantha Spade play the coming scene her own way. Shortly thereafter, he'd heard the tap-tap of her heels outside the door, without questioning how he knew it was her; he simply did.

The doorknob rattled. The door swung open on a squeaky hinge, admitting a cloud of fragrance: gardenia. Click-click went those heels, muffled after a few steps by the Oriental carpet.

Damn, he wanted to *see* this woman, but there was something at stake here and he wouldn't break first. The picture-postcard view of the city no longer registering, he waited.

And waited.

She laughed—chuckled, really, as if pleased. "Well, well," she said in a throaty voice that was almost a purr, "if it isn't Nicholas Charles, my number one insurance agent."

That "number one" label was a nice surprise. Nick turned warily. "And you are...?"

Her laughter turned raucous. "I knew I liked you, sweetheart. Come sit down and we'll talk turkey."

Nick couldn't sit down. If he tried to move, he'd trip over his astonishment.

Samantha Spade was *some woman*. He'd never seen her like before. Hell, she could be straight out of a forties film noir. This dame could hold her own with Bette Davis or Joan Crawford or Mary Astor or any of the rest of them.

She wore a gray suit with tailoring he envied— no blouse underneath, just a broad-shouldered jacket and a skirt that ended slightly below her knees. Ankle-strapped spike heels accentuated slim, silky-looking legs. While he continued to stare, she turned and walked to the desk located before a large window. He could hardly believe his eyes; there were *seams* up the back of her stockings.

She sat, leaning to open a drawer and haul out a bottle half-full of something that looked a lot like bourbon. "Drink?"

She sounded amused. Perfectly arched brows rose over eyes with lashes way out to there. High cheekbones gave her face a sculpted look and her mouth was an exaggerated slash of dark red lipstick.

She might be thirty-five, she might be...hell,

she might be sixty. Nick had never seen anyone so...ageless. He blinked, trying to focus his tired brain. She seemed such an anomaly, a woman out of time and place. Until he looked into those eyes and realized that *he* was the one out of time and place; this woman knew exactly who, what and where the bodies were buried.

"Drink?" she asked again, setting two squat glasses beside the bottle.

Nick cleared his throat. "I'll pass." He sat across from her in a straight-backed wooden chair.

She nodded. "Good idea. You don't look so hot at the moment." She poured a couple of inches into one glass and replaced the bottle in the drawer. "Good job on that last caper. Have a nice trip home?"

"Not particularly." He just wanted to sit there staring at her, trying to figure her out.

She didn't seem to mind. Indeed, she seemed perfectly at ease. She sipped her drink with appreciation. "Okay, that's enough idle chitchat," she announced. "I've got another assignment for you."

He groaned. "Since when do I get my assignments straight from the—"

"Horse's mouth?" she interrupted, carmine lips quirking up in a half smile.

"I was going to say, from the top."

"Better yet. To answer your question, this job is for a...special client."

"And that is...?"

"All in due time. First I want you to know why I picked you."

"Because I'm available?"

She grinned. "Because you're a smart-ass who won't be easily intimidated." Her brown eyes narrowed. "And because you're the best at thinking on your feet."

Brain currently functioning with all the agility of a bowl of mush, he was finding her *plenty* intimidating. "I'm flattered," he said after a significant pause.

"Yeah, I thought you might be." She stared into her glass, serious now. "This job will require a trip to Las Vegas—perhaps an extended trip."

"When?"

"Day after tomorrow."

"Jeez! Gimme a break here. I just finished the last job."

"Quit bellyachin'." She stung him with a scornful glance. "This is a gem of a job. *You* should be paying *me*."

"Yeah, sure." He rolled his eyes. "So what is it?"

"A stroll in the park. Practically a paid vacation. It's probably a false alarm, anyway. You're insurance, just in case."

"How long will it take?"

She shrugged. "Who knows? Your client will tell you when it's over."

He frowned. "That's pretty damn evasive. Don't you think you'd better tell me who this special client might be?"

For the first time, she didn't meet his gaze. "Hell," she muttered, "it might be me."

He curled his lip derisively. "Yeah, sure. Pardon me for belaboring the obvious, but I get the feeling you're a match for *anybody*. Why would a woman of your…*experience* need a bodyguard?"

"I'm not hiring you to guard *me*," she snapped. All the guile with which she'd been handling him slipped away. "I'm hiring you to guard the s.o.b. I plan to kill the minute I get my paws on him." She waited a few seconds for that to sink in before adding, "Sure you won't have that drink now?"

He took the drink.

1

THRILLED DOWN TO HER TOES, Cory Leblanc stared around the lobby of the exclusive resort outside Las Vegas, Nevada, wondering what the heck she was doing in Wonderland. She'd never seen such a fabulous place in real, as opposed to reel, life: all marble floors and mirrored walls and crystalline chandeliers. Curving glass walls soared from floor level to the ceiling three stories above, tinted to keep the unrelenting sunshine at bay.

It was like walking out of a furnace and onto the set of an MGM musical comedy—in magnificent Cinemascope and glorious Technicolor, yet. For an unworldly young woman who lived a monochromatic life, La Paloma Lodge was a stunner.

If Crystal could only see me now, Cory thought. *Yes!*

Even the Nevada anthem—the jingle of coins in slot machines—sounded glamorous in this setting. Bellhops hurrying past in their maroon-and-silver uniforms, little pillbox hats tilted over their foreheads, added to the musical comedy atmosphere.

Actually, Cory was waiting for just such a bellperson. He'd piled her luggage onto a cart along with that of several other lodge guests, then invited her to wait for him inside where it was cooler. She'd been more than happy to oblige.

She didn't mind waiting. She could *live* in this lobby.

A tanned young woman undulated past, her tight white dress dazzling. Cory followed the woman's progress until her glance stalled on a reflection of herself in the mirrored wall. She did a double take. Could that glamorous creature really be Corinne Leblanc? She might feel like a rank imposter, but thanks to her friend Crystal, she didn't look like one.

Not only was she newly blond and "permanently" curled, her makeup was polished and her summery dress perfectly appropriate to the setting. She had Crystal to thank for everything. She'd dragged Cory through half the shops of Houston, throwing money around as if either of them had it to throw.

But what the heck, Cory thought, her spirits soaring. This would probably be the only chance she ever had to see how the Beautiful People lived. So she didn't have a job; so she barely had a nickel to her name. What she *did* have was two glorious weeks of paid vacation at La Paloma Lodge, courtesy of her only uncle, a man whom she hadn't seen in years.

When her day in the Nevada sun was past, she'd scurry home to Texas and start pounding the pavement in search of gainful employment. But when she did, she'd be *darned* if she'd settle for another boring, dead-end job—or man—like those she'd left behind.

She craved romance! Adventure! There'd been

little of either in her first twenty-seven years, and she'd be darned if she'd blow what would probably be her last shot at either. No one knew her here, except Uncle Mario. No one knew how boring and uninteresting she really was, so maybe she could fool them for a couple of weeks.

Crystal, who was beautiful and sexy and popular with everybody, said that beneath Cory's dull exterior lurked a femme fatale just waiting to burst forth. Now that there was no one left to tell Cory what to do, or be hurt if she declined to do it, the time had come to turn that femme fatale loose.

The sound of running water slowly penetrated her concentration on her own astonishing image. Turning, she saw a waterfall streaming from the third floor to splash and dance in a reflecting pool in a niche to the right of the entryway. She breathed a soft "Ahh!" of appreciation and automatically took a step toward it, propelling herself directly into the path of a man just walking past.

Her shoulder bumped against his chest and she jumped back, embarrassed. "I'm so sorry," she began—and stopped short. The man who stood before her was the most gorgeous male she'd ever seen in her life, far better looking than those movie stars Crystal drooled over. And he was smiling at *her*, a friendly, interested kind of smile that said it was perfectly all right, she could run into him anytime.

His long-lashed blue eyes crinkled pleasantly. "My fault entirely," he said in a voice with no discernable accent. "Forgive *me*. Perhaps we'll run into each other again."

Lips parted, Cory stood there while he walked

around her to rejoin his companion. Together they approached the registration desk, two bell-persons dragging a mountain of luggage behind them.

All Cory could think was *My goodness, what a stunning couple.* The woman was tall and sleek and commanding, moving with utter confidence on stiletto-heeled, ankle-strapped sandals. Her broad-shouldered, sky blue suit fit like a coat of spray paint, not a wrinkle marring its smooth surface. She wore a perky, feathered blue hat with a tiny veil tilted over one eye.

Cory would have felt—and no doubt looked—like the class clown in such an outfit. Then she'd probably fall off those heels and break her neck. This woman, on the other hand, carried the look off with total aplomb.

The man of Cory's dreams spoke to the clerk, then lounged against the counter, waiting. His idle glance touched Cory's, lingered with…could that be interest? A shiver of surprise darted through her. That such a man would look twice at her was a thrill in and of itself. But this was the new, improved Cory Leblanc, she reminded herself. Lifting her chin to a determined angle, she looked right back at him.

Crystal would doubtless approve.

There was plenty to see, starting with thick black hair and challenging blue eyes. His curvy mouth had a sardonic tilt she liked. He was all decked out in classy sports clothes bearing designer labels, and the heavy gold watch gleaming on his wrist looked as if it must have cost a mint.

What was he to the woman—her son?

You wish, Cory scoffed at herself. The woman was older than him but not *that* much older. Besides, they looked and acted nothing alike: she was cold and elegant while he was warm and magnetic.

Nor were they relating like mother and son. Cory saw the woman reach out and stroke the man's cheek as if she owned him....

Which she probably did. Cory sighed. Just her luck; the first sexy guy she saw turned out to be a kept man.

"Sorry for the delay, miss." Her bellperson, a tall skinny kid with red hair, hustled up, dragging an overburdened luggage cart. "If you'd like to register now..."

Would she! She could stand in line right behind...the plump bald man in the Bermuda shorts and aloha shirt, for the good-looking couple was nowhere to be seen. Which didn't turn out to be too bad, actually. The portly gentleman announced that he was a cosmetic salesman from New York and promised her a selection of samples that would make her the envy of all she met.

Unfortunately, the only person she was interested in impressing had just disappeared with a Joan Crawford look-alike. Still, she had two whole weeks to find him again.

NICK DISMISSED the bellhop with a handful of dollar bills and turned back inside the two-bedroom bungalow he'd be sharing with his boss for the foreseeable future. Said boss stood at a window, flinging back the drapes and throwing the casement wide.

"I hate air-conditioning," she groused, taking a deep breath.

"Has it somehow escaped your notice that we're in a desert? If you turn off the air-conditioning we'll suffocate."

"Who said anything about turning anything off? I'm just opening the window." She spun around and headed for one of the two closed doors.

"Hold it!"

Samantha stopped but didn't turn, instead casting an arch glance over one broad shoulder. "I can only hope you're not speaking to *me* in that tone," she said in a dangerous voice.

"Damn straight I am." Nick walked past her to throw open the door that had been her destination. His cautious glance slid around the bedroom, done in whitewashed bamboo and bright exotic prints similar to those in the spacious sitting room. Crossing to the windows, he opened the drapes, revealing nothing but a great view of landscaped desert oasis.

Ditto the bathroom; a gnat couldn't hide beneath the blue-and-white glare of powerful fluorescent lighting. The second bedroom was equally innocent. Relaxing, Nick returned to the sitting room.

Samantha gave him another of those chilly looks. "Don't act like a mug," she said. "Nobody's going to get knocked off or anything like that. It's not that kind of deal. You're overreacting, gumshoe."

"Am I?" He shrugged. "Hard to be sure of that when you haven't told me what this is all about."

She eyed him coolly. Despite the heat of the Nevada desert just beyond the door and pouring through the open window, she looked like the proverbial cucumber. "I don't mind your little P.I. games, but I would appreciate it if you'd remember who's in charge here," she said.

"Sister, when I'm on a job *I'm* in charge."

She did a double take and he knew she was startled because he'd called her "sister." But hell, he'd seen an old movie or two in his lifetime. If it was good enough for Humphrey Bogart, it was good enough for Nicholas Charles.

She burst out laughing, which surprised him. She had a big laugh for such a sophisticated woman and he found himself smiling in response.

"Okay, sweetheart," she said, "I guess you can have it your way until I get enough and have to slap you back into line."

"Rhetorically speaking, of course."

"Of course." She didn't do "innocent" very well but she gave it her all. "Look," she continued, "why don't you scram—check the layout of this place or flirt with the girls or something. I could use a little peace and quiet."

"You sure? Maybe I should hang around and—"

"I'm sure." She made a shooing gesture toward the door. "I'm not used to being cooped up with anybody, if you want to know the truth. You're going to start getting on my nerves any minute now. Besides, you might pick up some good dope."

"Good dope?" He frowned, not understanding.

"Dope—scuttlebutt, scoop, information."

He grimaced. "I wouldn't know good dope if I stumbled over it."

"You could get lucky." She pointed. "I'll take that bedroom."

"Swell. I'll haul in your lug—"

"Get out!" Swinging around in the doorway, she glared at him, although the little hat tilting over one eye tended to lessen the impact. "I can carry my own valises."

"Jeez, you're a hard woman to get along with." He started for the door to the other bedroom.

She looked exasperated. "I told you to scram. What do you think you're doing?"

He glanced down at his khaki trousers. "It's too hot to wander around dressed like this." He darted her a critical glance. "Or like that."

"Who are you, my fashion consultant?"

"I thought I was your bodyguard, a fact you seem to have trouble remembering."

"Not likely, with you hanging around to remind me. Swell, change your clothes, whatever. Just don't bother me."

The door slammed. For a few moments, Nick stared at it, then he shrugged and went into his own room. She wasn't the first difficult client he'd worked with.

The worst, probably, but not the first.

HE HAD TO ADMIT, La Paloma Lodge was one helluva place. The massive main structure with its red tile roof included the airy lobby, several restaurants, a casino, and guest rooms and suites on the upper floors. Another dozen "guest complexes" made up of individual bungalows were arranged artfully around central courtyards landscaped with saguaros and other high-desert plants.

Alert to his surroundings, though careful to conceal his interest, Nick wandered past tennis courts—at least a dozen— past a health club with racquetball and spa facilities, past biking and hiking trails, even a croquet court.

He paused at a kids-only swimming pool to watch children of all ages zooming down the water slide through a tumbling waterfall. All were tanned and fit looking.

Squinting, he peered up through the lacy leaves of one of the hundreds of paloverde trees that provided shade if not coolness. Even the powerful sunglasses he wore seemed ineffectual against the glare of the sun in a cloudless blue sky.

Everything was in order. Time to reward himself with something tall and cool. Until Samantha decided to confide in him—if she ever did—there wasn't a helluva lot more he could do.

Through the trees to his right lay another swimming pool, that one for adults. He strolled toward it, hands thrust in the pockets of his khaki shorts. His pale blue polo shirt felt too warm, but his feet were comfortable in heavy strapped sandals. He wondered if Samantha would bow to reality and shed that suit.

He wondered why he wondered.

He paused at the gracefully curved edge of flagstones rimming the free-form pool. This was the life: some guests lounging in the sun, others in the shade, reading or napping or talking. Only a few hardy souls actually ventured into the water. For most of those, it was simply something to pass through to get to the man-made islands in the middle, there to lie on lounges while sipping frosty drinks.

Nothing suspicious here. Even so, he turned in a slow circle to be sure he'd checked everything out.

And then he saw her.

He blinked and his eyes widened. It was the woman who'd stepped into his path in the lobby, and she looked…hell, she looked better than Esther Williams in her movie heyday. Beautiful and blond, she stood on the ladder near the top rung of the one-meter diving board, staring out at the water with total concentration. Grabbing the top rail, she stepped up onto the board, the firm muscles of her arms and legs moving sleekly.

She wore a white, curiously old-fashioned-looking swimsuit. One-piece and perfectly plain, it did all kinds of nice things to her—or she to it. He'd never have guessed that kind of body lurked beneath the dress she'd been wearing in the lobby, although he'd noted her general attractiveness.

She sucked in a deep breath and her ribs arched below full breasts. Viewing her in three-quarter profile, he checked out details with a connoisseur's eye: narrow waist, flat stomach, long…*very* long and very shapely legs.

She'd tucked that mass of curling blond tendrils behind her ears, where it cascaded down around her shoulders, still dry. Her face displayed character as well as beauty, with a strong jaw and high cheekbones, a straight nose and wide forehead.

Watching her, Nick felt his stomach clench. Her concentration touched him in an almost physical way. She made a completely sensual picture, and his own reaction was a total surprise to him.

He wasn't here to ogle women. But on the other hand, if Samantha continued to shut him out, he'd need some kind of distraction. In which case, a babe like this one might be just the ticket.

A no-strings summer romance between two consenting adults, that was his style. Remembering the bold way she'd sized him up in the lobby, he figured it was probably her style, too.

Unexpectedly her concentration broke and she looked up with a question on her face. Her gaze locked with his. For an electric moment, they simply stared into each other's eyes.

She shook her head with a visible effort. Moving smoothly, she stepped into her hurdle and sprang from the very end of the board. With the grace of a ballerina, she stretched into a layout, more popularly known as a swan dive. Just for an instant he saw her perfectly posed against a blue sky. Then she stretched for the water in a vertical line.

Nick was no longer watching. Wearing only three items of clothing, he stripped off two of them and dove off the side of the pool.

What the hell. If Sam insisted on keeping him dangling, he might as well enjoy himself.

CORY LOVED TO DIVE. She'd been a competitive diver all through high school and college, because it was the only sport approved by her overprotective mother. Cory had kept it up as much as she could afterward, for the sheer pleasure. Those fleeting seconds of weightlessness at the apex of a dive always sent a surge of joy through her.

Which was why she'd headed for the pool as soon as she got settled in her small bungalow and ascertained that Uncle Mario was nowhere to be found. She was comfortable in the water, any water.

She'd felt shy taking off her flowered cover-up, although there was no reason she should. Competitive swimmers and divers certainly were accustomed to appearing in public in suits so thin and tight that they left absolutely nothing to the imagination. This suit might be plain, but it hadn't been built for speed. She didn't want to think about what it *had* been built for or she'd chicken out for sure.

So she'd lost herself in preparation for the dive, interrupted by *his* appearance. Even rattled, she ripped the entry; she could feel it. No splash, minimum surface disturbance. Twisting beneath the surface, she touched the bottom of the pool with her feet, bending her knees and preparing to push off.

She found herself looking into the blue eyes of the man she'd been fantasizing about ever since she'd seen him in the lobby. She blinked, thinking perhaps she was imagining things, then shoved drifting strands of hair away from her face for a better look.

He was still there on the bottom of the pool with her. He formed a circle with his thumb and index finger and mouthed the words *Good dive.* He gave her a charming, if watery, smile.

Flustered, she pushed off and shot to the surface. Without hesitation, she struck out for the side of the pool, stroking strongly. Hoisting herself up on her arms, she swung around to sit on the side.

He was nowhere to be seen.

Either she had imagined him or he was drowning. With a little gasp of alarm, she shoved off the edge, meaning to drop feet-first into the water.

Instead, she dropped feet-first into his arms as he popped up at the edge of the pool. They went under all in a tangle, water-slick bodies sliding intimately against each other. Cory came up coughing and choking.

He held her against his chest until she caught her breath. Then he said, "We've got to stop meeting this way."

That brought on a new spasm of coughing. When she could speak, she said around laughter, "Why? Aren't you tough enough to take it?"

Those beautiful blue eyes brimmed with humor. "I'm a lover, not a fighter."

"In that case," she said tartly, "we have nothing in common."

Disentangling herself from his grasp, she swam away from him, across the widest part of the pool. To her pleasure, he easily kept pace with her. His stroke was nothing fancy, but it was powerful.

Her feet struck the sloping bottom and she walked to the wide steps and out of the pool.

Tossing wet hair over her shoulders, she turned to wait for him—and saw he was wearing shorts, not swim trunks. She gave him a quizzical look. "You don't seem to be dressed for the occasion. Did somebody shove you in?"

He glanced down, looked surprised by his apparel. "That's one explanation, all right."

When she started to turn away to find her cover-up, he stopped her with a light hand on her forearm that she felt all the way to her shoulder. His touch was as potent as his appearance, all sleek and strong and confident. She swallowed hard and tried to think of something halfway intelligent to say.

He spared her the effort. "Can I buy you a drink?" He guided her toward the right side of the pool. "Let me grab the rest of my stuff and we can flag down a waiter."

"Oh, I don't know if that's—"

Cory Leblanc, she heard her friend Crystal shouting, *you're an idiot!* And it was true. You didn't find romance and adventure by turning down the best offer you were likely to get in this lifetime. Of course, he *could* be some kind of con man—and she already suspected he was a *kept man.*

But not for certain. "Sure," she said, swayed by curiosity as well as lust. "A drink sounds good." She felt bold and sophisticated and savvy.

"Great." He bent to pick up a shirt and a pair of sandals lying on the side of the pool, the muscles of his back gliding beneath the smooth brown skin. "Where would you like to sit?"

She pointed. "I left my stuff over there."

"That's what you think." A dimple appeared in his cheek. "You've got all your *good* stuff with you."

Pleased and embarrassed, she led the way to the table where she'd left her cover-up and rubber thong sandals. Slipping the flowered fabric over her head made her feel infinitely better. Until she turned toward him, anyway.

How did that go? *Undressing her with his eyes…* Fanciful but accurate. Not to mention flattering. Her breath caught and she looked away, spotted a waiter and waved him over.

"Name your poison," her companion invited.

"How about a…" she racked her brain "…white wine?"

He groaned. "Boring but acceptable. I'll have…" He, too, hesitated. "It's too hot to get serious. Bring me a margarita."

"Make it two, and forget the wine," Cory said quickly. She *was* boring, but she'd just as soon not advertise it.

The waiter departed. Nick pulled out a padded pool chair for her and she slipped into it gratefully, because her knees were shaking. "I don't think I've had a margarita since I was in college," she said, watching him towel off that lovely chest with his knit shirt.

"Not much of a drinker, huh?"

She wasn't much of an anything. She shrugged with studied nonchalance. "I've had my moments."

He sat down, stretching out those long strong legs. His wet shorts stuck to muscular thighs in soggy wrinkles, which he ignored. "Good."

She blinked. "Good?"

"I've had my moments, too, so I wouldn't want to hit on a sweet young thing. I do have my principles, after all."

She burst into delighted laughter. "Are you *hitting* on me?"

"I'm considering it." He grinned back. "Would I be taking undue advantage if I did?"

"Are you kidding?" She tried to look scornful of such a ridiculous idea.

"I hope so."

And then he just kept looking at her in that quizzical manner, making her want to shift nervously in her chair. He must be remembering her clumsy arrival into his life in the lobby. So much for her impersonation of a sophisticate.

He opened his mouth to speak but she beat him to it. "Yes," she interrupted. "I'm the woman who bumped into you in the lobby a couple of hours ago."

"You think I don't know that?"

"Oh." Surprised and flustered, she rushed on. "And now I've almost drowned you. If you were smart, you'd probably avoid me."

"Probably. Do you have a name? I like to know who I'm avoiding, or hitting on, as the case may be."

She grinned ruefully. "We haven't been properly introduced, have we?" She stuck out her hand. "I'm Cory Leblanc of Houston, Texas—actually Corinne, but nobody's named Corinne anymore."

"I don't know why not. It's a pretty name." He

took her hand in his, and again she felt that tingle. "I'm Nicholas Charles—Nick to my friends."

"I'm glad to meet you, Nick." Eventually she remembered to withdraw her hand. "And you're from…?"

"Here, there, everywhere."

"I see." She didn't, but that was beside the point. "I've never been to Nevada before," she continued. "My uncle invited me but we haven't connected yet." This was Nick's cue to tell her about the beautiful older woman who'd entered the lobby with him.

He obviously wasn't good at taking hints. "So until this uncle materializes, you're on your own?"

"Well…yes." She wasn't sure why she was so reluctant to admit that, but she was. Maybe she didn't want him to think she was so without charm that she had to vacation alone or with relatives.

"I enjoyed watching you dive. You're damn good."

"Thanks." Praise always embarrassed her. "So what do you—"

"Drinks are here." He lifted two frosty glasses with salty rims from the waiter's tray, passing one to her. Quickly he signed the receipt, then picked up his drink. "Cheers."

"Cheers." She sampled her margarita, the salt and lime juice tart on her tongue. *Ohh*, she could get used to this!

"So," he said, setting his glass on the white enamel tabletop, "what do you do in Houston, Texas, Cory?"

"I used to work for an insurance company."

Was that astonishment on his face? Whatever it was, he covered it quickly. "Used to?"

"I just quit. When I get home I'll be looking for a new job." And a new man. And a new life.

"You don't look sorry about that."

"I'm not! Scared, maybe, but not sorry." She leaned forward, for some reason eager to confide in him. "Insurance is so boring. I want to do something more—more exciting."

"Such as?"

"I don't know." She knew she was speaking too freely to this stranger, but when he turned his sexy blue gaze on her, she felt as if she'd been hit by a truth ray. "Maybe something physical. I could teach swimming and diving to kids. Or maybe I'll join the army. Or I could—I don't know, become a detective or join the police force. I just want something interesting, for a change."

"Insurance to private eye…now that's quite a stretch."

"You're laughing at me."

"I'm trying hard *not* to laugh at you," he said, but his words didn't sting. In fact, his expression was warm and approving. "Your enthusiasm's inspiring, Cory. Maybe—"

He broke off, his gaze caught by something beyond her. Twisting in her chair, she saw what had grabbed his attention.

It was the woman he'd arrived with, walking along one of the curving paths toward them. *Holy cow*, Cory thought, she was still wearing the suit and heels. She should be steaming in the sunshine, yet from here she looked cool and unrumpled.

"It's your friend," Cory said.

"Yes." He half rose, his palms against the tabletop. He looked angry. Or maybe he looked disgusted.

"She's very beautiful." Cory could barely contain an envious sigh.

"I suppose."

She could almost feel his tension. What was going on here?

He straightened abruptly. "If you'll excuse me, I'd better see what's on her mind. It's been nice talking to you, Cory."

"You, too." She also rose, trying to mask her disappointment. "Thanks for the drink." Was that all he had to say? No dinner invitation, not even one of those all-purpose excuses that would let her down easy? So much for her new image. *Thank you very much, Crystal!*

"Perhaps we'll run into each other again."

Ah, the all-purpose let-her-down-easy phrase she'd been expecting. "Maybe." She made it noncommittal, because he'd hurt her feelings.

"Or maybe—damn!"

While she was still blinking in surprise, he leaped over a pool chair and raced off at top speed. Staring after him openmouthed as she was, it took Cory a moment to realize why.

The woman he'd been watching had just been intercepted by a man—a man who suddenly swept her into his arms and kissed her.

2

NICK SPRINTED TOWARD Samantha, arms and legs pumping. His lapse in surveillance infuriated him. What the hell kind of bodyguard was he, anyway? Okay, Sam wasn't exactly cooperating, but he should never have left her alone.

Since he had, it was up to him to teach this amorous jerk a lesson. Nobody was going to manhandle Samantha Spade and get away with it while Nick Charles was on the job. He'd have to make a real serious example of this guy.

Grabbing the man by the collar, Nick hauled him away from Samantha, who, on closer observation, didn't appear to be struggling all that hard to escape. Hauling back his right arm, Nick made a fist and prepared to loosen a few teeth.

"Hold it right there, buster!"

He pulled up on the punch. "Damn it, Samantha, since when do you let every Tom, Dick and Harry accost—"

"That's no Tom, Dick or Harry. That's my husband, Joel Caspar." She sounded almost amused. "Turn him loose."

"Your *husband?*" Nick's jaw dropped and he stared at the man still constrained by his iron hand. This trim, gray-haired guy didn't exactly look like a mugger, that much was true. And on second glance, he *did* look a great deal like one of the men whose photograph Nick had seen in the San Francisco office.

Samantha smoothed down her suit jacket. "Ex-husband, if you want to get technical. Which part of 'turn the man loose' don't you understand, Nicholas?"

Nick unclenched his hold and let the man settle back onto his feet. "Sorry about that," he said, although he was still seething. His condemning gaze turned on his boss. "You care to explain this?"

"Not particularly." She ignored him to speak to her ex. "Are you all right, sweetheart?"

The man shrugged. He was about the same size as Nick, who hung in right about six feet, and he had a certain easygoing way about him when he wasn't being threatened.

"No damage done," Joel responded as cheerfully as if he got jumped every day. "You must be Nick Charles. Samantha's told me almost nothing about you." He stuck out his hand.

Nick shook it without enthusiasm. "I'm a little confused, here," he said, giving Samantha a pointed glance. It was an understatement.

"You jumped to a false conclusion."

"*Jumped?* He who hesitates can end up dead."

"Don't quote my own book to me."

"Damn it, Samantha!"

"Yours is not to reason why, precious." Her red mouth quirked up at one corner. "Did I mention that Joel owns La Paloma?"

Nick bit off a groan. "No. What else haven't you mentioned?"

She slid an arm around Joel's waist. "Have I mentioned we've remained very close since the divorce?"

"No, but I've got eyes." Nick shoved a hand through his hair. "Do you really think it's fair to—"

"Nick!" Samantha's gaze narrowed. "You might introduce your friend."

"My...?" Nick glanced around to find Cory fidgeting nearby, an expression of concern on her face. Her hair was drying in a mass of ringlets and she looked absolutely adorable. He felt himself soften and fought it. He'd been ignoring business while pursuing pleasure, never a good idea. Still...he'd enjoyed flirting with Cory and could imagine doing considerably more than that.

He gestured for her to approach, which she did with some hesitation.

"Is everything all right?" she asked. "You took off so suddenly...."

Samantha gave that throaty, knowing laugh. "All a misunderstanding, I can assure you." She stuck out a hand. "I'm Samantha Spade. And you are...?"

"Cory Leblanc." Cory put her hand into Samantha's much more competent-looking one. "That's Corinne, actually."

"I'm pleased to meet any friends of Nicholas."

"I'm not actually a friend," Cory objected. "We just met. He bought me a drink."

"I see. He picked you up."

"Actually," Cory snapped back, "I picked *him* up. It's a nineties thing."

Nick nearly choked on a burst of laughter. It

was good to see someone hold her own with the acid-tongued Ms. Spade. He touched Cory's elbow to indicate his support. "She's from Texas," he said, as if that explained everything.

"Everybody's got to be from somewhere." Samantha raised one brow. "Are you here alone, Miss Leblanc?"

"I am." Cory looked the other woman right in the eye. "I'm meeting my uncle, but he hasn't shown up yet."

"In that case, you must join us for dinner."

Cory glanced quickly at Nick. "I wouldn't want to intrude."

"You won't. Joel, you'll join us, too, of course."

"Of course." He saluted her with a dip of his chin. "Have I ever refused you anything, Sammy?"

Nick's stomach clenched. He'd been warned his first day of employment with S. J. Spade Insurance that one called the boss lady "Sam" or "Sammy" on pain of death. He waited for her to belt the fresh ex-husband who'd already played fast and loose with her person.

She just smiled fondly and said, "Some things never change," before returning her attention to Cory. "Nicholas will collect you at eight."

"I could meet you in the dining room," Cory said quickly. "There's no need—"

"He'll be delighted to do it, won't you, Nicholas."

"Delighted," he agreed. He liked Cory Leblanc of Houston, Texas. But equally important, he was annoyed with Samantha for neglecting to mention an ex-husband. To Nick, this indicated a dangerous tendency to withhold vital information.

But what the hell. She was the boss. He'd just have to outsmart her from here on out. If she thought to distract him with the presence of Cory Leblanc, she had a big surprise coming.

SAMANTHA POURED the martinis. "Your new friend Cory seems somewhat insipid," she mused, "which should make her quite amenable to anything you have in mind."

"Insipid, my aunt Gertrude."

"There's no uncle, of course. Or if there is, he's more a sugar-daddy-type uncle."

"That's a hell of an imagination you've got there—and don't change the subject." Nick was getting a little hot under the collar, but reined it in. "We were talking about a dangerous tendency on your part to withhold vital information." Nick, who didn't love martinis, took one and drank. "Samantha, you know I can't protect you if you don't level with me."

She savored her own drink before responding. She was already dressed for dinner in a long white gown of some fabric that clung to her impressive body. Iridescent white sequins in a flower design curved over one broad shoulder and across both breasts.

She looked like a million bucks. She sounded like a broken record. "I told you, I'm not the one who needs protection." Walking to the window, she pulled aside the patterned curtain and glanced out. Despite the fact that the air-conditioning was blasting out cold air, the window was open. "I'm simply pleased you've already found someone to…amuse you while we're here, even if she is a rather common type. Perhaps your little blond bombshell will keep you from making a mountain out of what is most likely a molehill."

"Amuse me. Yeah." But he hadn't missed the "most likely." Which meant Samantha wasn't sure herself what they were facing. "About your ex-husband—"

"Joel has nothing to do with our reasons for being here," she said quickly. She glanced at the gold-and-diamond watch glittering on her wrist. "Run along now and pick up Miss Leblanc."

"What about you? You're my first priority, especially—"

A knock on the bungalow door interrupted him. Samantha smiled. "Joel will take excellent care of me," she said, "and there he is now. We'll meet you later in the dining room. And Nicholas…" She regarded him with shuttered eyes. "Take your time."

He left fuming. He didn't like being treated like a schoolkid sent on his way with a pat on the head.

CORY COULDN'T HELP feeling a bit like Cinderella in her glamorous new dress and the fancy evening makeup Crystal had gone to such pains to teach her to use. Batting long mascara-covered lashes into a mirror, Cory gave her reflection a tentative smile.

She might look different on the outside, at least to herself, but inside she was still that little wallflower, Corinne Leblanc. Crystal was trying to make a silk purse out of a sow's ear.

Was such a thing possible? But if not, why was Cory waiting for the knock of a megahunk upon her door?

Because he'd been ordered here by his…what? Friend? Relative? Lover? Whatever she might be to him, Samantha Spade was a woman obviously accustomed to having her own way. Despite her faintly scornful manner, she wanted Cory to be there at dinner tonight—and there was no mistaking that whatever Samantha wanted, that's what she'd get.

Maybe Nick really didn't mind the invitation, Cory mused, trying to encourage herself. He had acted interested when they'd shared that drink beside the pool—not to mention during their encounter *in* the pool. It had been quite a shock to look into his handsome face and feel the force of that blue gaze even underwater. But the way he'd reacted when Mr. Caspar kissed Ms. Spade had not gone unnoticed by Corinne Leblanc.

Nick's outrage toward Mr. Caspar could very well be jealousy. Cory sighed with regret. She'd come here looking for romance and adventure, and Nick Charles had appeared almost as if on cue. If he was "otherwise involved," she'd have to keep looking. But if Ms. Spade took up with her ex again, maybe…just maybe…

Cory groaned. How much "romance" did she really want? Would she sleep with Nick, a nearly perfect stranger in more ways than one, if she got the chance? Her heart pounded at the suddenness of that thought—and the fact that she didn't immediately reject it.

Did she have the nerve? Maybe she'd be better off just avoiding him and enjoying her luxurious surroundings until she could hook up with Uncle Mario. She glanced with pleasure around the small bungalow he'd arranged for her.

Decorated in the colors of a desert sunset, it was compact but inviting. She even had her own patio, looking out at the magnificent grounds.

Even so, all she could think about was Nick, who certainly appeared to be the answer to a maiden's prayers. Nick, a man who *didn't* look as if he were a stranger to romance...and maybe even adventure.

What she needed was a shot of self-confidence. Turning to the telephone, she dialed Crystal's number.

NICK KNOCKED ON Cory's door at precisely 8:00 p.m. She opened it so quickly that he figured she must have been standing just inside, waiting for him. She seemed so guileless, yet looked so sophisticated. It was a tricky balancing act, but she handled it with aplomb.

"I hope I'm not early," he said, knowing perfectly well that he wasn't. Then he did a double take.

Cory wore a dress almost identical to Samantha's, except it was baby blue and minus the sequins. While Samantha's hair was coiffed in a series of dark rolls and waves, Cory's golden curls spilled across her shoulders. He didn't realize he was staring until her hazel eyes widened.

"What is it?" she asked. "Is my slip hanging? Do I have lipstick on my teeth? You look so...shocked."

He pulled himself together. "Maybe it's because you look so different than you did at the pool, or in the lobby, for that matter. I hardly recognize you."

She stepped back to allow him to enter. "Is that bad? I can change. Maybe this dress isn't appropriate?"

"The dress," he said flatly, "is great. Don't change a thing for me."

"Are you sure?" She didn't look convinced.

"More than sure. You're gorgeous."

"Thank you." Her cheeks actually turned pink. She was the picture of innocence. "I'm ready, if you'd like to go," she added.

"There's no rush." He moved farther into the room. "I hoped you'd offer me a drink."

"I'm afraid I have nothing to offer." She seemed genuinely disappointed.

"If that's true, you must be a heavy drinker." He crossed to the entertainment unit on one side of the room. Opening a door, he revealed a small refrigerator. "We'll find something in here, guaranteed."

She looked delighted. "I didn't know that was there!"

"Obviously. So what'll it be? Screwdriver, Bloody Mary, booze with soda or tonic, beer—"

"Screwdriver, I guess."

"And I'll have a beer." He pulled out the premixed drink and the beer and closed the refrigerator door. Lifting cubes from the ice bucket into a glass, he poured her drink and handed it to her. He opened his beer and lifted it, still in the bottle, in a salute. "Cheers," he said. "This could be the start of a beautiful friendship."

She smiled and repeated, "Cheers!"

They drank. Intensely aware of her in the sexy blue dress, he glanced deliberately around the room. Her one-room bungalow was smaller than the one he shared with Samantha, but the decor was the same. "Nice," he said.

"I even have a patio." She watched him through a lowered fringe of lashes.

"May I see it?"

"Of course."

She led the way around the bed to billowing sheer curtains and drew them aside. He threw open the sliding glass doors and stepped through. The patio was larger than he'd expected, with room for two chaise longues and a small matching table between. Walls of some material that looked like carved rock separated the patio from its neighbors and provided privacy. Flowering vines spilled over the top from built-in containers.

She took a deep breath, her breasts rising sharply beneath soft fabric. "Don't the flowers smell wonderful?"

He breathed deeply. "Something smells wonderful, but I'm not sure if it's the flowers or you—your perfume."

"My…?" Her hand flew to her throat and her gaze locked with his.

He stepped closer. "You're wearing perfume, aren't you?"

"Yes." Her voice turned throaty, sexy.

"Let me check this out."

He bent his head toward her shoulder and she automatically turned her head aside, offering him exactly what he wanted. Moving so close to her that he could feel the heat of her skin, he drew in the scent of flowers...and woman.

"It's you," he murmured.

She shivered and he knew she'd felt the warmth of his breath against her neck.

"I overdid the perfume." She licked her lips. As if remembering that nothing held her rooted to the spot, she took a quick step away.

He followed, as he was sure she intended. "You didn't overdo anything. You look great and you smell good enough to eat."

She gave him a tremulous smile. "Stop that," she said without conviction.

"Stop what?"

"Flirting with me."

"You don't like it?"

"I like it all right, but..." She seemed to struggle for words. "I don't know you. I'm not used to taking up with strangers."

"I can provide references."

"I'm afraid that by the time they arrive, it'll be too late."

Nick thought so, too. Smiling, he put his beer bottle on the table, then placed his hands on her shoulders. "I guess you'll just have to trust me, then." He cupped his hand beneath her chin and gently raised her face.

She sighed, long lashes drifting down. "You think that's easy?"

"Easy as pie. Just make up your mind. Say, 'I, Cory Leblanc—'"

"I, Cory Leblanc—"

"'—do hereby resolve to trust Nicholas Charles—"

She repeated his words.

"—who is a fine, upstanding gentleman graciously dedicated to making this a vacation to remember.'"

She laughed, but dutifully said the words back to him.

"We could seal our pact with blood, but I know a better way," he said, and kissed her.

Or tried to. The moment his lips touched hers, the crash of glass sent them bolting apart. Cory had dropped her drink, which smashed on the indoor-outdoor carpet as if against marble.

For an instant, they stared at each other. Then Nick grinned. "Moving too fast?" he asked.

"M-maybe just a little." She drew a trembling breath. "I really think we should go now."

"If you insist on being sensible."

She smiled and some of the tension seemed to leave her. "I'll just find something to clean up this mess first."

"We'll ask someone to come take care of that."

"Oh, of course. Good idea." She met his gaze, her own contrite. "Did my drink splash on you?"

He glanced down at black tuxedo trouser legs. "No."

"Me, either." She didn't smile. "We were lucky, I guess."

Yeah, he thought, *lucky. You're either the most innocent woman I've ever met or the most devious, Cory.*

And if it's the second, you're good. You're very, very good....

HE'D BEEN ABOUT TO KISS her, and she had to go and drop her glass like an idiot! If he never tried again, she'd have only herself to blame.

Everything had been going so well. Glancing obliquely at him as the plush elevator carried them swiftly to the top floor of the main building, she wondered what he really thought about her. Had she been too forward? Had she been too shy? Had she been *boring?*

The elevator door slid open with a soft whir and they stepped out into a carpeted foyer decorated with the muted elegance she was coming to expect here. When Nick took her arm, she felt just like the heroine of that Technicolor movie she'd fantasized about: bright, sophisticated and very, very interesting.

He steered her toward the sound of music, stopping abruptly just outside a huge arched entry. He looked stunned.

"What is it?" she asked. "Is something wrong?"

"That's a rumba band in there. How retro can you get?"

"I think it's kind of nice," she said uncertainly. "Different, but..." She saw Samantha Spade and Joel Caspar coming toward them and stopped speaking to stare. The elegant and sophisticated Ms. Spade wore a dress so similar to her own that all Cory could do was gasp and mutter, "Oh, my gosh!"

Samantha stopped short, her dark eyes narrowing dangerously. "Well, well," she murmured, "what have we here?"

Nick tightened his grip on Cory's arm. "Obviously two women with excellent taste," he said. "Joel." The two men shook hands warily.

Samantha squared those broad shoulders. "Who could argue with that?" She swept past them and through the arched entryway, Joel at her heels.

Cory cast a helpless glance at Nick, but he just smiled, shrugged and guided her forward.

They walked into a huge, old-fashioned nightclub, where small, linen-swathed tables were terraced around a sunken marble dance floor. A band on a stage at one end, the musicians wearing those funny shirts with ruffled sleeves, and bright handkerchiefs around their necks, was playing to a full house.

"I'm dreaming." Cory clutched Nick's arm. "I've never seen anything like this, at least in real life."

"Who has?" He mouthed the words, adding, "Stiff upper lip, okay?"

That seemed the only course of action as they followed Samantha and Joel toward one of the tables—actually, the best of the best. It was located just in front of a potted palm, close to the dance floor, but not so close that the music would blast away all conversation.

Tuxedoed waiters appeared, pulling out chairs, presenting wine lists and menus; busboys filled crystal water goblets. Cory tried to go with the flow, although she felt more out of place than ever. But why should she? At Crystal's urging, she'd made a conscious decision to break out of the rut in which she'd lived her life. No matter what happened, she vowed she'd never regret taking this chance.

How many ordinary, everyday people got the opportunity to rub elbows with the elite? That's what Cory was doing, sitting here with the most handsome man she'd ever met, the wealthy owner of one of the most elegant and luxurious lodges in the country, and a woman…how to describe Samantha Spade? A woman more handsome, more intimidating, more sophisticated and assured than any Cory had ever met.

Maybe she should take on Ms. Spade as a role model.

"You're smiling." Nick spoke softly. "Why?"

"Because I suddenly realize this is one night in a million and I'm going to enjoy it."

She thought she saw understanding on his face.

"Good for you, but I doubt it's going to be just one in a million. Maybe…six in a million? How long are you staying at La Paloma?"

"Two weeks."

"Then eleven or twelve in a million, at least."

Samantha leaned across the table, rapping smartly with the knuckles of one hand. Diamonds sparkled on her wrist. "What are you two whispering about?" she demanded.

"Nothing," Cory said quickly.

"Then pay attention." Samantha's smooth brow remained unfurrowed. "I forgive you for wearing my dress."

"You…?" Cory blinked, belatedly realizing what a ridiculous statement that was. "Then I forgive you, too," she said grandly, "even if yours is prettier. The sequins are a nice touch."

"That's true. And white's a better color than that blue, but still…" Samantha drew an exasperated sigh. "This has never happened to me before. I trust it never will again."

"Not if I can help it," Cory said.

WHEN CORY "FORGAVE" Samantha for wearing the same dress, Nick thought he'd fall out of his chair. He felt considerable satisfaction that Cory was holding her own with his formidable boss.

As the evening progressed, he found himself watching Cory instead of paying attention to the byplay between his boss and her ex, which he should have been doing in hopes of picking up a clue to the mystery surrounding this trip. The wine steward served champagne—very expensive champagne selected by Joel—and Nick's enjoyment of such a rare vintage was heightened by Cory's pleasure. Good lord, he actually expected her to say the bubbles tickled her nose.

She apparently enjoyed the caviar a bit less, nibbling only a tiny bit on a cracker. When the waiter appeared to take their dinner order, she hesitated, then ordered lobster.

It wasn't difficult to coax her onto the dance floor while they waited for their food. By then the Latin sounds had been replaced by a dance band with a smooth mix of forties tunes. Cory moved into his arms a bit awkwardly.

"What a lovely evening," she said with a sigh.

"It's not over yet," he said, trying to find their rhythm. "We haven't even had dinner."

"I know, but champagne, caviar, music and dancing..." She stumbled, stepped on his foot and gasped. "I'm sorry! Oh, I'm such a klutz. I've never been a good dancer. I should have warned you that I have two left feet."

"No, you don't. You're just tense, for some reason." He coaxed her with a smile. "I don't bite. Relax and let yourself follow me."

She gave him a wary glance, but tried to do as he directed. Within seconds, they were moving smoothly to the music.

She looked up at him with surprise on her lovely face. "Is that all there is to it? Just...relax?"

"Sure." He spoke with a double layer of meaning. "That's all there is to a lot of things. Relax...and enjoy."

"I think I can manage that." She missed everything but the obvious—or seemed to.

They danced for a few minutes in a charged silence. With each movement, they became more synchronized, until he held her so closely that they truly moved as one.

Damn, she felt good pressed against him this way. He slid the hand he'd placed between her shoulder blades down until he was touching her waist. With subtle pressure, he pulled her closer.

She was going to be here two weeks. A lot could happen in two weeks.

Of course, *he* might only be here for twenty-four hours—or twenty-four days, who knew? Maybe nobody knew, including Samantha. She was deliberately vague when he brought up the subject. Hell, she was deliberately vague when he brought up any—

Nick stopped in midstep.

Cory faltered and looked up. "Did I trip you? And I thought we were doing so well."

"Shh—we are."

Something was wrong. He stared past her to the table where Joel and Samantha sat sipping champagne and quietly chatting. What had disturbed him so? Nick wondered. Something was wrong...out of place.

Could it be the man in the tuxedo stopping behind Samantha's chair, then leaning down to kiss the back of her neck?

3

NICK BARRELED OFF the crowded dance floor with a roar, leaving Cory staring after him and wondering what had happened now. And she'd been doing so well, she consoled herself. She hadn't stepped on his feet in...minutes.

Lifting her dress to her knees, she sprinted after him.

"Nick Charles, get your paws off that man!" Samantha rose from the table in all her fury, while Joel Caspar just sat there looking stunned.

Nick, getting right in the stranger's face, roared back at her. "Damn it, Samantha, if you tell me this is another one of your long-lost ex-husbands—"

"Bingo!" Samantha's chilly voice cut through his tirade.

Nick did a double take, then slanted a quick glower at Joel, who shrugged. "I thought *he* was your husband."

"They're both my husbands—or ex-husbands, if you want to get picky. Nicholas, the man you're strangling is Wil Archer, my first husband."

"Jeez," Nick groaned, "how many more husbands have you got wandering around out there? Because I'm getting damn sick and tired of playing this game." But he released the man he'd been holding a virtual captive.

"None," she said. "There were only three and the second one died years ago. You have my permission to beat the hell out of the next stranger who makes a pass at me." Suddenly the beautiful and self-possessed Samantha Spade seemed to crumble. "Oh, Wil," she murmured in a voice that threatened to break, "what are *you* doing here? Is it because of…" She caught her breath, hesitated, then threw herself into the arms of her first ex-husband, the man who'd come upon the scene second to her third ex-husband.

Cory thought it all terribly romantic.

If confusing.

NICK, STILL HOT under the collar, sure would have liked hearing the answer to the question posed by Samantha: what *was* Wil Archer doing at La Paloma? But a straight answer did not appear to be forthcoming.

"We'll talk about that later, Sammy," the newcomer said, his tone wary. Patting her shoulder, he trained a narrow-eyed gaze on Nick, to whom he spoke in a gravelly voice. "And you are…?"

Nick Charles," he answered, "I'm a close friend of your ex-wife's," he added for the hell of it.

At Nick's shoulder, Cory leaned in. "And I'm Cory Leblanc, a friend of everybody's," she said.

Samantha gave a final snuffle against Wil Archer's chest and straightened. Her face was pale; obviously, his appearance really *had* been a helluva a shock to her. She glared at Archer. "You might have told me," she croaked accusingly.

"Precious, I had no idea you'd be here," he said, the soul of reason. He looked tired and a little ragged around the edges. His hazel eyes were bloodshot and deep creases etched his cheeks. "I just checked in a half hour ago and decided to grab a bite to eat—"

"So you put on your tuxedo?" Nick was not amused and didn't care who knew it. "Sammy" was playing him for a sap—again.

Archer shrugged. "Old habits die hard," he said. "Sammy, let's take a powder. We have plenty to talk about."

"God, yes. After all these years!" Her crimson lips trembled. "Excuse us, all. Wil and I have a lot of…catching up to do."

Nick dug in his heels. "You just ordered dinner. What are we supposed to do with it?"

"Eat it, angel." Samantha gave him a look chilling in its sweetness. "Just *eat* it."

"Sammy." Archer gave her a reproachful glance.

"Sorry." She lifted one perfect brow. "If you don't want to eat it, Nicholas sweetheart, you can—never mind. We're out of here."

And they were.

Nick glared after them, feeling like a fool all over again. Hell, he couldn't tell the players without a scorecard, and no one had offered him one of those.

CORY ENJOYED HER LOBSTER.

She couldn't help it, even if Nick only poked at his steak, while Joel Caspar shoved his plate aside entirely and concentrated on the champagne.

Both men looked dark as thunderclouds. It occurred to her that they were jealous of Wil Archer.

How depressing. It must be nice to have three attractive men vying for your favor. Of course, one of the three was nearly young enough to be Samantha's son.

Meoww! Cory was ashamed of herself for such a thought. Appetite appeased, she leaned forward on her elbows.

"Well, Mr. Caspar—"

"Joel," he said, tossing back his champagne.

"Joel. Thank you. I was about to say I admire the way Ms. Spade remained friends with her ex-husbands. Not many women could pull that off."

"Not many women are in Samantha's league," he said. He stood up abruptly. "If you'll excuse me, I have a few things to take care of. I'm sure I'll see you again before you leave."

"Of—" Before she could add "course," he was gone. She turned to Nick with a frown. "Was it something I said?"

"Yeah, probably." He glanced at her plate, which was practically devoid of edible morsels. "Let's get out of here."

Her heart leaped. "You mean together?"

He grinned for the first time since he'd spotted Samantha's second, or was it first, ex-husband. "Yes, together."

"Sure! Where shall we go?"

"We could check out the casino. How does that sound?"

"You mean gamble?"

"That's what most people do in a casino."

She laughed. "I've never gambled. Not even a quarter in a slot machine."

"Then we'll rely on beginner's luck." Rising, he caught her hand and pulled her up after him. "I need a distraction and you're it."

Glad to be "it," she followed him happily from the club.

HOURS LATER in front of her bungalow, Cory turned to Nick. Her hazel eyes were half-closed and a sweet little smile curved her lips as she slumped back against the front door.

He smiled back at her, thinking that he'd never known a more complicated woman. Not even Samantha Spade could match the conflicting signals he got from this one. One minute he thought she was a sophisticate playing games and the next he thought she was an innocent without a clue.

It was crucial that he figure out which was the real Cory, because it was no strings or nothing. He had no intention of leaving any broken hearts or bad feelings behind him when this asinine assignment was over.

She licked her lips and the action sent a little jab of awareness through him. "What time is it?" she murmured.

He didn't glance at his watch. "About four."

"In the *morning*?" She groaned and let her head fall back against the door, her eyes drifting completely closed. Long lashes lay on her cheeks like delicate fans. "Did we wind up in the chips?"

"We broke even." Actually they hadn't, but the few hundred dollars they'd lost would go onto his expense account—thank you very much, *Sammy*.

"That's a relief." Cory lifted a hand to stifle a yawn. Both strappy sandals dangled from the other hand. "Excuse me. That was sleepy, not bored. I'm not used to such late hours."

"Does this mean you're not going to invite me in for a drink?" He was teasing her. He was tired, too, and eager to get back to his own digs. Which he could safely do, now that the bellhop he'd paid to tell him when the lights went off in Samantha's bedroom had reported in.

Cory opened her eyes a crack. "If I had one more drink, I'd keel over," she predicted.

"We wouldn't want that. May I have your key?"

The hazel eyes opened all the way this time. "But I said—"

"I have to see you safe inside before I go," he explained patiently.

"Oh." She looked disappointed.

Rummaging inside her small black bag, she extracted a flat plastic rectangle. He took it, inserted it into the lock and opened the door with a quick twist. Then he stepped aside to let her enter, thinking that he was just about the noblest son of a bitch who ever lived.

Truth was, he couldn't take the chance of going inside that room with its dominating damn bed. He just couldn't be sure about her. One minute she was flirting with him, the next she was blushing and stammering like a schoolgirl. He didn't know *what* the hell to make of her. Until he was sure what kind of woman she was, he didn't intend to take any chances. No matter how intriguing...attractive...desirable he found her....

"Thanks for everything." She stopped in the doorway, turning toward him again. "I'm sorry to be such a drag."

"You're not a drag."

"Then why aren't you kissing me good-night?"

Oh, hell. "Because you're a little bit tipsy, and a little bit sleepy, and I'm not sure you know what you're doing."

"You couldn't be more wrong," she murmured. "I know *exactly* what I'm doing."

She put her hands on his chest beneath the tuxedo coat, sliding them up to his shoulders. With her drowsy gaze locked with his, she rose on her toes and put her lips against his.

Tentatively...cautiously...while every muscle in his body went rigid. Her fingers dug into his shoulders and she sighed, a soft sound that jangled along his nerve endings like a siren. Deliberately—it had to be deliberate; it couldn't be an accident—she pushed his jacket aside and pressed her breasts against his chest, her arms twining around his neck.

But her mouth remained closed, her lips warm and soft and...damn it, kind of innocent somehow. Finally she pulled back and gave him one more sleepy smile, said a sweet, "Thanks for a lovely evening," stepped inside her room and closed the door gently in his face.

And there he stood alone in the courtyard, hard as a rock and twice as dumb. Swearing under his breath, he turned and hobbled away.

WITH THE CLOSING OF her door, Cory collapsed against it in a trembling mass. She couldn't believe what she'd just done—but she couldn't deny she'd done it.

She'd deliberately tried to tempt Nick Charles, stranger that he was, into kissing her. Unfortunately, he hadn't succumbed to her charms. Ha! Her charms. She staggered across the room, faint with reaction, and fell upon her bed. Since he wouldn't kiss her, she'd kissed him!

At the last minute, she'd kind of chickened out, though. That peck could hardly be called a kiss. On the other hand, if it wasn't a kiss, why was she a mass of sensation from head to toes?

He was without a doubt the sexiest man she'd ever met! Pressing her knuckles against her teeth, she stared out at the moonlit patio beyond the glass wall. She'd wanted adventure and romance and she'd gone after it. If she never saw him again, at least she'd know she'd tried.

She'd try again tomorrow, if she got the chance. In the meantime…

Rolling off the bed, she stumbled into the bathroom and turned on the water for a shower.

A *cold* shower.

Then, even if it meant waking her friend from a sound sleep, she'd call Crystal and beg for guidance.

ALL SIGNS OF vulnerability were absent from Samantha's face and demeanor the following morning.

Nick, who'd been sipping coffee in the sitting room while waiting for her, felt a ripple of unease.

Once he'd left Cory, he'd spent the better part of last night trying to figure out Samantha's emotional reaction to seeing Wil Archer again. He'd come up empty.

Now here stood Samantha, crisp and controlled in a navy blue-and-white-flowered dress and the ubiquitous ankle-strapped shoes. Not a hair was out of place, not a wrinkle of concern marred her face.

"I could use a cup of joe," she said.

Nick provided coffee without comment. Only after she'd had that first reviving gulp did he speak. "Either you tell me what's going on or I'm out of here," he said. It wasn't a threat, it was a promise.

She knew it, too. Balancing her cup and saucer, she took the settee opposite him. For a few moments she looked at him with a brooding expression. Then she sighed. "I'll tell you what I can," she said. "If it's not enough…"

He understood. Nodding, he settled back in his padded bamboo chair to listen.

"Don't get too comfortable," she suggested wryly, though it was obviously difficult for her to go on. "This isn't going to take long. You see…many years ago, Wil and I suffered…a great loss. Unfortunately, we couldn't agree on how to handle it. Those differences led to the dissolution of our marriage, after which I stayed in San Francisco and Wil relocated to London."

"And you haven't seen each other since…until yesterday?" No wonder she'd looked so shocked!

She took a sip of coffee before answering. "That's right."

"And the loss you shared…?"

She looked away. "I can't discuss that with you, Nick. It's not that I won't, it's that I can't. I've…been warned to keep my trap shut."

"By…?"

She shook her head sharply.

"But whatever brought both of you to La Paloma has something to do with that loss," he ventured.

She chewed on her bottom lip. "Possibly."

"So now I've met your first husband and your third husband. Someone told me that you'd inherited the agency from your second husband."

"Somebody talks too much." Her amber eyes flashed. "When I pay salaries, I expect loyalty."

"Are you kidding? The people who work for you are a bunch of clams. I think that's the only bit of information about you that's common knowledge. Anyway, I'm guessing that in San Francisco, you met your second husband at what was then simply a detective agency when you went to him for help with the problem that broke up your marriage."

"I'll neither confirm nor deny that."

"And I'd guess that he wasn't able to solve your 'problem' and now it's come back to haunt you—you and your first husband. You're both here for the same reason. Am I right?"

She stood abruptly. "That's enough guessing. Go dally with your little friend and let me sort this out on my own. If I need you, I'll call you."

"Hell, Sammy," he drawled, "now that Archer's here you don't think you *will* need me. But you're wrong. A fresh pair of eyes is exactly what you need. If you and Archer couldn't handle it the first time, what makes you think you'll be able to handle it now?''

She stared at him, lips parted, breathing lightly. He could almost see hope mingled with fear of fresh disappointment warring in her expression. Then she said, "This time we have a clue."

NICK ATE LUNCH by the pool, reading the *Wall Street Journal* and brooding over his unsatisfactory conversation with Samantha and the unfulfilling manner of his parting from Cory last night. When Cory herself appeared on the walkway coming from the direction of the health club, he steeled himself to avoid speaking to her or even catching her eye.

Why court trouble? Until she passed by, he'd keep his head buried in the paper and—

"Hi, Cory. Where are you off to in such a hurry?"

She paused at the edge of the pool, gorgeous in a red T-shirt and white shorts that emphasized those fabulous legs, a towel thrown over her shoulders. After a moment's hesitation, she approached his table.

She didn't smile. "Hi," she said. "You wanted something?"

"You—to sit down."

She blinked. "Oh. Sure." She plopped into the padded patio chair and looked at him expectantly. With her blond curls caught up in a ponytail and her face glowing with perspiration, she looked fresh and radiant and all of sixteen years old.

She was also quite obviously distracted. "Is something wrong?" he inquired. "When I took you to your door last night—"

She blushed and looked away. "I'm sorry about that," she murmured.

"I'm not." He grinned and it nearly cracked his face. He hadn't done much smiling so far today.

She looked dubious. "I'm glad to hear it." She fiddled with the hem of her T-shirt. "Nothing's wrong, exactly. It's just that I can't locate my uncle Mario."

"The one who brought you here."

She nodded. "He was supposed to leave a message at the desk for me, but he hasn't. So I called the casino where he said he works—"

"Said?"

"Yes. They've never heard of Mario Moretti. At least, that's what the man told me."

She really seemed anxious about it. "Maybe there's just been a mix-up," Nick suggested. "Are you sure you called the right casino? There are hundreds in Nevada, you know."

"I'm sure."

"Which one?"

"It's called The Fat Man's." She wrinkled that straight little nose distastefully. "Classy, huh!"

Nick felt a shiver of unease. The Fat Man's was known as a hangout for the darker element in Las Vegas—petty hoods, wise guys, hookers and assorted other undesirables. Uncle Mario was probably not a nice man, if that's where he worked.

Nick saw no reason to share that with the man's niece, however. "I don't think you have anything to worry about," he said, soothing her.

"Something probably came up. He'll get in touch with you eventually."

"I hope so. If he doesn't…" She shrugged. "I'll go into town and try to track him down tomorrow. I might get more information if I talk to the people at The Fat Man's face-to-face."

"If you decide to do that, let me go with you."

Her eyes widened. "Why?"

"Because you don't know Vegas. It's not the kind of town where a woman should be wandering around alone." She looked doubtful, so he added, "Besides, I've got a rental car. That's simpler than calling a cab."

"If you say so."

He relaxed a bit. "Where were you heading when I called you?"

"Inside for lunch. I've been working out in the weight room and trying to figure out what might have become of Uncle Mario."

"Have lunch with me," he invited, indicating a half-eaten hamburger growing cold on his plate.

She glanced around. "Won't Ms. Spade be joining you?"

"Ms. Spade is dining with Mr. Archer."

Her brows rose. "Does that upset you?"

She thinks I'm jealous, he realized. He gave her a reassuring smile. He'd known that, sooner or later, he'd probably have to tell her something about his relationship with Samantha. The truth was out of the question, so he dredged up the lie he and Samantha had agreed upon.

"Wouldn't it upset *you* if you thought your uncle was making a big mistake?"

"Yes, but…" Cory stared at him. "Ms. Spade is your aunt?"

"Bingo!"

"But…" She frowned. "You didn't know your own aunt's marital history?"

Jeez, how much had she overheard during the confrontations with Samantha's two exes? "Aunt by marriage," he improvised. "I knew she was the Auntie Mame of the family, but some of the details are a little foggy."

Cory looked relieved. "That's great! I mean, family's important."

"What about *your* family?" he asked, neatly changing the subject.

"All gone except Uncle Mario," she said sadly. "My mother died eight years ago, when I was nineteen, and my father only a few months ago. I haven't seen Uncle Mario since Mom's funeral, or heard from him until he invited me here."

"That's strange."

"I thought so. I mean, out of a clear blue sky, I get a letter from him with tickets and reservations, the whole nine yards." A huge smile curved her lips. "He couldn't possibly have imagined how his generous gift would change my life."

A thousand possibilities, all bad, flooded Nick's mind. "Change your life? You just got here."

"It changed before I even got on the plane. But I don't want to bore you with my personal history."

She started to rise and he caught her hand, stopping her with a smile. "I'm very interested in your personal history," he objected. "Order a hamburger and tell me all about it."

She made a few objections, but he got his own way. By the time they'd finished lunch, he'd learned a great deal about Corinne Leblanc. More than she realized.

He knew that she'd been a dutiful daughter to an invalid mother who was extremely protective of her only child, keeping Cory much too close during her school years. Only after Rhea Moretti Leblanc's death and Cory's graduation from college with an English major, had Cory planned the biggest gamble in her life: a move to New York City. Over her father's objections, she insisted on staying with her college friends and finding a job in publishing.

Her rebellion was short-lived. Andre Leblanc suffered a heart attack six days before she was to leave for New York. Of course, she'd given up her dreams and stayed home to nurse him back to health. She'd gotten a job at the same large insurance company where her father worked, to make him happy and to keep an eye on him.

"His recovery was never complete. He died a little more than two months ago...." she ended finally.

Nick watched and listened as her voice trailed off. "There's more," he guessed.

She sighed. "Are you sure I'm not boring you?"

He was very sure. He nodded.

"I was engaged to a man my father thought was perfect for me," she said. "I was working in a job my father thought was perfect for me—until marriage, of course, and then I'd stay home and take care of my children."

"Am I hearing past tense here?"

She laughed grimly. "You're quick, I'll say that for you. Yes, past tense—the day after I heard from Uncle Mario, I quit my job and broke my engagement."

"And now you're sorry," he guessed.

"Oh, no!" the words exploded from her. "I don't want the job—never did. I took it for Daddy's sake. As for the man…" She rolled her eyes. "Let's just say he deserved better than me."

"I doubt that."

"It's true. He deserves someone who loves him, not someone who wants…who wants…"

"What, Cory? What do you want?"

"I've already told you that. I want romance and adventure. Failing that…" Her sweet mouth curved up at both corners. "Failing that, I'm going to find another job and start over, and this time I'll live my own life."

"Sounds like a plan."

"A *good* plan," she agreed. "I'm really on my own for the first time in my life, and I'm going to make the most of it. No more boring insurance for me."

Her determined gaze locked with his and he felt that almost imperceptible jolt of empathy. Ms. Corinne Leblanc was determined to kick up her heels, and the man she wanted to kick them up with was Nick Charles.

Who might or might not be strong enough to stick to his resolve to mess around only with

women who knew the score. Because he understood now, beyond a shadow of a doubt, which
Cory was the real thing, the genuine ingenue.

And a damn shame it was.

4

THEY PLAYED TENNIS that afternoon—Cory won—
and then they swam together in the blue lagoon
that doubled as a pool. After drinks at the pool-
side bar, they parted, promising to meet in the
lobby at seven for dinner and perhaps another
shot at the slot machines.

Nick berated himself for being an idiot all the
way back to the bungalow. Each minute they
spent together made him more aware that this
was *not* the best use of his time, yet he found himself curiously powerless to step aside and let her
seek "adventure and romance" with some other
guy.

Hell, this could actually be a good exercise in
self-control. And Nicholas Charles was a man
who prided himself on self-control. So it *might* be
a little difficult to give her adventure and romance without sleeping with her. So what?

He'd make up his mind right here and now that
no matter what happened he would *not* make
love to Cory Leblanc.

The decision was made. He could relax.

Fitting the plastic card key in the slot, he
opened the front door of the bungalow just as Samantha walked out of her bedroom. She wore
white pleated shorts and a white blouse tied up

over her midriff, all that white setting off the beautiful golden color of her skin.

Cory had skin just about that same color. It practically glowed, and he wasn't sure how much that had to do with the sun and how much with her natural coloring. Cory's hair was blond, while Samantha's was dark, her eyes hazel instead of brown… He shook his head sharply, wondering why the hell he was still thinking of Cory.

Samantha spoke sharply. "Don't take that attitude with me."

He frowned. "What attitude?"

"*That* attitude—that superior attitude."

"I got news for you, boss. I wasn't even thinking about you."

For a second she looked disbelieving. Then understanding dawned. "Ms. Leblanc, is it? Good."

"Think so?" He crossed to the small bar refrigerator and pulled out a can of fruit juice. After popping the tab, he took a deep swallow.

"She's keeping the boy occupied," Samantha commented tartly. "Are you having dinner with her tonight?"

"Not if you're available. Lady, I'd feel a helluva lot better if you'd let me hang around with you."

Her expression softened. "I don't need you when I have Wil and Joel. You may as well have a little fun, too, sweetheart."

"What the hell are we waiting around here for, anyway?"

She grew still, poised there in the doorway. "I don't know yet," she said finally. "I'll know when it happens."

"Son of a—" He bit off the curse and turned toward his room. "Okay, you're the boss. But if this blows up in your face, it may be too late for me to do anything about it."

"I'm beginning to suspect that nothing's *going* to happen. This could all be a terrible joke." She placed one forearm over her bare midriff as if in actual pain. "Look, we'll stay here for two weeks. If the case doesn't break by then, we'll go back to San Francisco and act as if nothing ever happened. In the meantime, court Ms. Leblanc, bed Ms. Leblanc, do any damn thing you want to do with and to Ms. Leblanc. Just don't worry about *me*."

"Yeah, I know. Worry about the bastard who's got you so stirred up that if you ever get your hands on him he's a dead pigeon."

She smiled as if in anticipation. "You're an angel," she said. "You really do understand."

He understood the chill running down his spine. Whoever put that feral gleam in Samantha Spade's eyes would be wise not to fall into her clutches. If he did, he'd be lucky to escape with his life even if Nick Charles *was* charged with his safety.

CORY AND NICK ATE, they drank, they danced and they gambled, and then they went back to her bungalow. By then, Nick was becoming acutely aware of his own limitations as a man of steel. It was all he could do to keep his hands off her.

She gave him a look that he interpreted to mean she sensed his struggle. "Want to come in?"

Hell, no, he wanted to go check on Samantha.

"Sure," he said, following Cory inside. "But just for a minute. I've got to—"

She turned so abruptly that she was in his arms before he knew what was happening. She smiled.

"Thank you for everything," she said. "This is the best vacation I've ever had, even if I *can't* find Uncle Mario."

With one arm around her waist, he brushed silky blond curls away from her forehead. "Tomorrow I'll help you track him down."

Her entire face glowed. "That would be wonderful."

"We'll go to the casino where he works. I'm sure someone can give us a lead." Vividly aware of her lower body pressed against his, he stood perfectly still, not wanting to start something he had no intention of finishing.

"That's a good idea." She was staring at his mouth. Lifting her arms, she slid her hands over his shoulders. "Nick..." Her laugh sounded husky and nervous. "W-would you like a drink?"

"I'm not very thirsty." He caressed her cheek with the back of his hand, tempted by the softness of her skin. Leaning forward, he pressed his lips to her temple.

She caught a shuddery little breath and her breasts brushed against his chest. "I'm afraid that's all I have to offer you," she murmured, "except..." She pulled back to look into his face, her gaze questioning.

He responded by tilting her chin and covering her mouth with his. Her lips parted willingly and he slipped his tongue into the wet heat of her mouth.

Holding her tightly, he walked her backward without breaking the kiss until he had her wedged up against a wall. He covered her breasts with his hands, feeling the nipples spring to life. Her quick intake of breath came only a second before she leaned into his grasp. Somehow his thigh was between hers, even hampered by the narrow skirt of her linen dress, and he felt himself growing hard and hot.

He slid his mouth from hers, gasping for air, then tickled her arched throat with tiny kisses. In another second he was going to—

He thrust himself away from her and the wall against which she slumped. His heart pounded and his pulse raced. Staring into that flushed face surrounded by a tumble of blond silk, lusting after those soft lips, he struggled to remember why he was even *in* Las Vegas.

It was because of a woman, but not this woman. He dredged up a crooked smile. "How about meeting me tomorrow at eleven in the lobby? We'll go into Las Vegas and nose around a bit."

She drew a shuddering breath. "That will be fine."

He edged toward the door, escape on his mind. "Unless something comes up, of course."

"Of course."

"Until tomorrow, then." He gave her a brief salute with one hand and slipped out the door, closing it gently behind him.

And asked himself what the hell had happened to his firm resolve.

YES!

Alone inside her room, Cory wrapped her arms around her waist and shivered. He wanted her. That sexy, handsome, sophisticated man wanted *her*, Corinne Leblanc of Houston, Texas. She could hardly believe her good fortune, although Crystal had predicted it last night on the telephone.

If he hadn't pulled back, Cory wouldn't have, either. She moved around the room, undressing, taking off the careful makeup and slipping into a sexy new black nightgown, repeating the pep talk she'd gotten from Crystal.

Cory wasn't the kind of woman who fell into bed with every man who indicated an interest— although there weren't that many who *had* indicated interest, if she was being honest. She didn't know much about Nick Charles; in fact, she knew nothing about him except that he was handsome and charming. She could hardly believe she was already thinking of sleeping with him, but she was.

Scowling, she went out onto her patio and leaned against the iron railing. Lights twinkled in the trees, and in the distance she would see the neon glow of Las Vegas against the horizon.

Crystal would laugh and say, "Go for it!"

Cory wanted to. She'd never been so attracted to a man and felt confident that she never would again. Of *course* she'd sleep with him if she got the chance. She was a grown and independent woman, after all, and she knew what she wanted.

She'd gamble to get it, too.

Appropriate for Nevada.

NICK HANDLED the red convertible like a sports car, slipping through bumper-to-bumper traffic with ease. He gave her an amused glance. "So what do you think of Las Vegas?" he asked.

She couldn't stop smiling. "It's just like I thought it would be."

"Tawdry and garish?"

She laughed. "Glamorous and exciting! I've never seen so much neon in my life."

"Nobody has," he said solemnly. "It's a tribute to the worship of greed."

She made a face at him. "Don't be so negative. I think it's very interesting."

"Different strokes." He maneuvered the vehicle into the right-hand lane. "Okay, we turn at the next corner if I've got my directions right. The Fat Man's is off the Strip."

The Strip, the famous Las Vegas Strip. Even that sounded glamorous to Cory. How could anyone be immune to all this: hotels and casinos featuring everything from the MGM lion to a reproduction of the New York City skyline, with knights and noble Romans and a circus thrown in. Marquees shouted the names of world-famous entertainers, and throngs of people and cars added to the holiday atmosphere.

The Fat Man's was a letdown after all the glitzy hubbub of the Strip, but even that modest establishment had more than its fair share of neon. Pulling into the parking lot, Nick killed the engine and turned to Cory.

"Ready?"

She was ready. Uncle Mario was responsible for her even being here, so she certainly owed him her thanks. And now that she thought about it, he owed her something, too: an explanation.

NOBODY KNEW ANYTHING. Nobody even admitted *knowing* anyone named Mario Moretti, and certainly no one by that name had ever worked at The Fat Man's.

"I don't get it," Cory complained. She and Nick stood in the middle of the casino after being ushered politely but firmly from the manager's office. The ding of coins hitting the metal payoff returns echoed around them, and cigarette smoke filled the air. "I know this is where my father said Uncle Mario worked."

Nick didn't want to point out that they'd just been given the bum's rush. No need to upset her unnecessarily. "Are you worried about your uncle?" he asked. "Do you think something might have happened to him?"

She considered. She looked slim and sexy today in a silky pants outfit that clung in all the right places. "No," she said finally. "Even when my mother was alive, sometimes we didn't hear from him for years. I suppose it's idle curiosity, but I'm dying to know why he wanted me to come here in the first place."

"He didn't explain?"

She shook her head and the soft curls bounced. "He just said it was important. And under the circumstances…" Her expression turned brooding.

"We can always go to the police if you're worried," he reminded her.

"That would just embarrass him. I'm sure I'll hear from him when he's good and ready—"

A shriek interrupted her, a woman's shriek of delight that sent a warning shiver down Nick's spine.

He'd know that sound anywhere! But what was Jennifer Jordan, Hollywood's flavor of the month, doing in a dive like this?

He turned, already in a defensive posture. There she was, rushing toward him, wearing oversize dark glasses with a scarf covering most of her glorious red hair. But she couldn't disguise that body: tall, long legged and big breasted, displayed by a skintight, midriff-baring T-shirt and tight black pants.

She flew into his arms. "Nicky! Darling, I haven't seen you since you saved—"

He kissed her. It was the only way he could think of to keep her from spilling the beans: that he'd been assigned to guard her delectable body almost two years ago. Actually, he *had* saved her from a gang of would-be kidnappers.

She'd rewarded him handsomely.

Very handsomely.

He came up for air and saw Cory staring at him as if he'd lost his marbles. Jennifer stared at him, too, as confused as anyone.

"But Nicky, if it hadn't been for you and Samantha, I could have been—"

He kissed her again; hell, there was nothing else to do. This time she wrapped her arms around his neck and kissed him back.

While he, poor sap, worried about how Cory was going to take this. He came up for air again.

Jennifer flashed her famous smile. "Really,

Nicky, I knew you'd be glad to see me, but this is ridiculous! I just wanted to—"

He made another move to stop her the hard way, but she feinted to one side.

"I wanted you to know that I eloped—that's why I'm hiding out in a dive like this. *I got married yesterday.* That's my husband over there glaring at you."

Nick released her in a hurry. "Sorry about that," he said, aware that his grin felt sheepish. He stuck out his hand to the curly haired guy glowering at him. "Your wife and I are old friends," he added lamely.

"Yeah, I see that." The glower didn't falter; the hand didn't rise.

Nick indicated Cory. "This is my friend, Cory Leblanc. Cory, this is—"

"Shh!" Jennifer put a finger to her lips and looked around quickly. "Don't say my name."

Cory looked annoyed. "I don't know your name," she said.

"You don't…!" Jennifer whipped off the glasses and snatched the scarf from her hair, all that liquid flame running amok.

Cory's eyes widened. "Oh, my God!" For an instant, she pressed her fingers to her astonished mouth. "You're—"

"Shh!" Jennifer tried to replace what she'd removed, fumbling a moment too long.

"Look, George, that's Jennifer Jordan!"

"Oh, Margaret, you're always seeing things— my gosh, you're right!"

Jennifer darted an accusatory glance at Cory.

"See? They know who I am. Don't you go to movies?"

"Look, look, it's Jennifer Jordan, the movie star!"

Jennifer, the scarf haphazardly tied on her head again and dark glasses hanging off one ear, looked stricken. "Nicky!" she appealed to him. "Do something!"

He held up his hands and shook his head. "Wish I could help, sweetheart, but you've got a husband now. Let *him* help you."

"I've had husbands before and none of them *ever* helped me," she yelled, turning to sprint toward the carpeted stairs. The curly haired guy trailed along behind her, a sullen expression on his handsome face.

Behind them streamed the fans, materializing as if from thin air. Nick had to turn away to keep from laughing.

"Let's go," he said to Cory.

"That was Jennifer Jordan!"

He took her arm and hurried her along against the flow of the crowd. "That's right."

"You know movie stars?"

"Doesn't everyone?"

"*I* don't." She didn't seem to realize how tongue-in-cheek his comment was. "What was she trying to say? You saved her from—what?"

They reached the front door to the casino and pushed through onto the sidewalk. There he turned and put his hands on her shoulders. "I saved her from boredom," he said, "which is what I'm prepared to do for you. If you'd like me to, of course."

Her full lips curved up in the most enticing way. "I'd like you to...if you have time, what with your aunt and all."

"She's pretty much tossed me out to fend for myself," he said, striving to sound pitiful and deprived. "Let's find someplace we can get a cup of coffee and check the telephone book. Then we can decide what to do next to find your uncle Mario. Sound good?"

Her eager nod said it sounded *real* good.

THEY CALLED EVERY LISTING in the Las Vegas phone book under "Moretti" and turned up nothing.

"So how far do you want to go with this?" Nick asked. They were sitting in a booth at a coffee shop, sipping iced tea and considering the options.

Cory sighed. "I don't know. I mean, what else *can* I do?"

"Plenty," he said, "but only if you want to. First tell me, would you call your uncle eccentric?"

"With a capital *e.*"

"Then it's not so far-fetched that he'd choose his own time to appear."

She considered. "Actually, it'd be just like him."

"Will your vacation be ruined if you don't see him?"

"No," she said again, thinking that Nick had the power to ruin her vacation, not Mario.

"In that case..." He spread his hands and shrugged.

Her conscience eased, she smiled. "Nick, you're incredible. Now if I could just figure *you* out."

He pretended modesty. "What you see…"

"No way! At first I thought you were an athlete—"

"Good God! Why would you think that?"

"Because of the way you moved when you thought those men were making passes at your aunt. But then I saw you reading the *Wall Street Journal* and decided you must be a businessman."

"The way your mind works is fascinating."

"When that movie star rushed up, I decided you must be in the movie business…but the way you've helped me look for Uncle Mario, I'm wondering now if you're…I don't know, a detective or maybe a newspaper reporter?"

In the process of swallowing tea, Nick sputtered. "Now I've heard everything."

"So which is it, or did I miss entirely?"

He looked thoughtful. "You don't really want to know," he said.

She stared at him. "Because it's something awful?"

"Because it's something mundane. Why don't we just say I'm a jack-of-all-trades and let you keep your girlish illusions? We've got a good thing going here. Why let 'real life' get in our way?"

Why, indeed? Staring into his mesmerizing blue eyes, Cory couldn't think of a single reason.

She was sure Crystal wouldn't be able to, either.

Cory and Nick returned to the resort late that night after doing the town and taking in a show. A message waited for her at the desk, and she read it aloud to him:

> "Hi, kid, glad you made it in. I had to go out of town but maybe I'll get back before you return to Texas. If I don't, you have a good time and don't worry about anything. I'll be in touch.
>
> > Your loving Uncle,
> > Mario"

Cory looked at Nick with concern. "That's funny," she said.

"What's funny?" he asked, curious to know how much of a coincidence she saw in Mario's note.

"That he'd pay all that money to get me here and then not show up to at least let me thank him."

"Sounds like he's a busy man." And a well-connected man. Obviously, someone at The Fat Man's had told Mario she'd been around asking questions. "You can still go to the cops about this."

She shook her head. "No, especially now that I know he's all right. I'm just going to do what he says—enjoy myself and hope he gets back before I have to leave."

"Whatever you say." Nick felt a certain amount of relief at her decision. Cops asking questions was one of his least favorite things.

She dropped her gaze. "Would you like to come to my place for a...drink or something?"

"Yes." He could see the half smile curving the corners of her mouth. "But I'm not going to. It's late. Want to meet for breakfast tomorrow?"

She looked disappointed, but nodded. "By the pool?"

"Sounds like a plan." He leaned over to kiss the tip of her nose.

She caught his hand and squeezed it. "Thank you again, Nick. I seem to be saying that a lot."

"My pleasure." Her hand lay warm on his wrist; he could feel his pulse hammering beneath her fingertips and wondered if she felt it, too.

"Sometimes two weeks seem like a lifetime," she said softly. Her gaze rose to meet his. "From this minute on, I'm not going to think about Uncle Mario or Texas or...or anything except having a great time."

"Good advice." Nick lifted her hand, turned it over and kissed her palm. "Want more good advice?"

She nodded, licking her lips. She was making this damn hard on him.

"Protect yourself in the clinches," he said. "Don't let things go farther or faster than you want them to—with me or anybody else. All the memories you take away from this trip should be good ones but...things happen. Sometimes the flesh is weak."

"Your flesh or mine?" Slipping her hand from his, she kissed her own fingertips and placed the kiss squarely on his mouth.

He stood there staring until her door closed behind her. Then he returned to his own bungalow and his own problems.

FOR THE FIRST NINE DAYS, nothing happened.

Nothing, except Nick thought he was going to burst if he didn't get Cory into the sack. Not that she appeared to have a problem with that, herself. Every time he touched her, she melted into his arms as if she'd just been waiting.

And therein lay the rub. Bedding her would be like taking candy from a baby.

Samantha provided little in the way of distraction. She spent all her time with one or the other of her ex-husbands—sometimes both. The reasons that had brought her here. whatever they were, appeared to be forgotten. She seemed almost as intent as Cory upon simply having a good time and putting all her cares and woes behind her. Even occasional calls from S. J. Spade Insurance Agency failed to disrupt what was beginning to feel a lot like a vacation—period.

The tenth day of togetherness was much like the others. Nick and Cory played—poorly—in a golf tournament in the morning, then spent the afternoon lounging around the pool. After dinner and dancing at the lodge, they found themselves once more before Cory's door.

Cory knew that Nick was finding it harder and harder to walk away. Each encounter carried them a little closer to the intimacy they both craved. Now he took her into his arms and kissed her, his hands moving unerringly to her breasts. At the same time, he pressed her back against the door with his hips against hers, letting her feel his arousal. If he hoped that would scare her off, he was in for a disappointment. She responded instantly, opening her mouth to him, pushing back boldly.

Urged on by Crystal, she found it had become like a little game—to see how far they could go without going all the way to bed. It was a game that was driving Cory mad.

"Nicky," she whispered against his mouth, "do you have to go?"

"Yeah, I'd better." He lowered his hands until they surrounded her waist, lifting her bodily until he could bury his face in the cleft between breasts exposed by the low-cut evening gown.

Gasping, she clutched him with her thighs. Letting her head roll back against the door, she fought to catch her breath. "Please...come inside," she gasped. "Someone will see us out here."

"Would that bother you?"

Not nearly as much as it would bother her if he left.

He nudged the top edge of her bodice down with his chin. Beneath it, she'd worn the sheerest nothing of a bra she could find among her new finery, hoping something just like this would happen.

When he sucked one nipple into his mouth, bra and all, she cried out sharply, then bit her lip. She didn't want to do anything that would cause him to stop. Nothing in her life had ever felt so good. He circled the nipple with the tip of his tongue, flicked the stiff point, then sucked it deep into the hot recess of his mouth.

She felt his hand on her thigh like a brand. The core of her had turned into a molten pool that grew hotter and deeper with each liberty he took. He circled her thigh with his hand, his fingers skimming under her skirt and over the slick nylon until they could rise no higher. At last his hand curved over the mound of curls between her legs and he began a sensual massage through the nylon barrier.

She thought she'd die if he lifted her any higher, and then he stopped and she thought she'd die for sure. Collapsed against the door, panting, disheveled, she stared at him. "What happened?" she gasped. "Did I do something wrong?"

"Not you, me," he said in a strangled voice. "I've got to get out of here before I do something we'll regret."

She pulled the edges of her gown over her breasts. Her nipples were so distended that they hurt. "I wouldn't regret it." She lifted her chin stubbornly.

"You might. If not now, later, and for the rest of your life."

She swallowed hard. "Now I'm really confused. What do you want from me? What do you expect?"

"Let's talk about it some other time."

"But—"

"Not *now*, Cory."

She watched him go, wondering how she was going to get her own way.

Wondering what she was going to do if she couldn't.

That's when her downcast gaze zeroed in on his silver money clip, lying on the walk near her feet. Carrying it inside, she stared at it blankly, wondering how she was going to solve her problem.

Because as a seductress, she was batting a big fat zero. She reached for the telephone and dialed Crystal's number.

NICK CHARLES WAS AN IDIOT.

He had to be, to keep tying himself up in knots over her night after night. Crossing the grounds toward his bungalow, he berated himself with every step.

Hell, he *wanted* to make love to her—had come very close to doing so before this—but he liked her too much to send her winging back to Texas like a wounded dove. Despite her outward appearance, she was a babe in the woods, and she was falling for him. *Too bad*, he thought savagely. When Samantha gave the green light, he'd walk away from Cory without a backward glance.

Damn it, he *would!* He just didn't want to hurt her, if he could avoid it.

He wasn't surprised to see his own bungalow dark. It was barely ten o'clock, the earliest he and Cory had parted since they'd met. Samantha had told him she'd be out late this evening, so he'd have the place to himself.

Opening the front door, he stepped inside and paused to get his bearings. Moonlight cascaded through open windows, laying out a silvery beam that was almost as bright as day, and soft desert air caressed his cheek.

Everything in the room was exactly as he'd last seen it; Samantha was nothing if not neat.

Dragging off his tie, he tossed it over the settee to make a sloppy statement, then turned toward his own room. His groin throbbed; he felt lousy. If he didn't get laid soon—

The soft sound of something hitting the floor in Samantha's dark bedroom brought Nick to a quivering halt. Every sense flared, came alert. He stood there halfway across the room, waiting.

A faint light suddenly glowed beneath the door, followed by the sound of a drawer opening and closing. Someone was obviously in there, someone who shouldn't be. A burglar, or the man-woman-or-child who'd lured Samantha to Nevada?

Whoever it was, a sense of elation swept over Nick. Action at last! He'd even welcome some good old-fashioned fisticuffs, if it came to that. Take out a few of his frustrations.

Damn few.

Walking lightly on the balls of his feet, he approached Samantha's room…reached for the knob…turned it with slow deliberation…threw open the door.

He was ready for anything—anything except the sight that greeted him.

5

SAMANTHA LAY PROPPED UP by several pillows on the bed, a sheet puddled around her waist. A thin trail of smoke rose from the cigarette between her fingers, and she tapped ashes into the ashtray balanced between her breasts. Wil Archer sat on the edge of the bed, looking back over his shoulder at her.

They were both naked as the day they were born. Nick, entering in a fighting stance, staggered back a couple of steps and groaned.

Neither Samantha nor Wil moved, other than to look at the intruder. The problem—and the embarrassment—was all Nick's. He started out strong, then quickly ran into trouble. "Jeez, I thought—you said—how was I to know? Damn, I'm *sorry*. I had no idea...." He backed toward the other room, hoping they'd allow him to slink away.

"Hold it." Samantha stubbed out the cigarette. Lifting the ashtray, she sat up, pulling the sheet over her breasts and tucking it beneath her arms. "Wait for us out there, Nicky. We need to talk."

"Yeah, okay." He added incongruously, "I never saw you smoke before."

"It's a nasty habit," she said. "I only do it after

sex." She raised one eyebrow. "Which explains why you've never—"

"I'll wait outside," Nick interrupted hastily, and fled.

SAMANTHA EMERGED five minutes later wearing a striped robe of some shiny material belted around her waist. She'd wrapped a white turban around her hair, and she wore those old-fashioned slippers without backs but with fluffy feathers on the toes.

Wil Archer was equally well turned out in a burgundy-colored jacket—jeez, was that what they used to call a smoking jacket? Nick cleared his throat. "I'm really sorry about that," he said, gesturing with his chin toward the open door and the unmade bed beyond it.

One of Samantha's eyebrows shot up. "If you'd busted in five minutes earlier, you'd have been sorrier." She glanced at her companion.

"Martini?" he asked, as if reading her mind.

Samantha nodded and sat on the small sofa. "Nick, I think it's time I told you what this is all about."

Nick felt a great load lifting from his shoulders. At last! He nodded, taking the bamboo chair opposite her. She didn't go on until she received her martini and took a gulp. Then she said, "Wil and I were married in San Francisco in—well, a long time ago." She darted her ex-husband an oblique glance. "Would you agree we were very much in love?"

Sitting beside her, he patted her knee. "That's

putting it mildly," he said in a tone at once gentle and gravelly.

Samantha's chin drooped. "A couple of years later, we had a child—a daughter. My God, we were beside ourselves with joy! We named her Laura."

Stunned by this news, Nick leaned forward. "I had no idea you had a child. What—?" He cut off the inquiry, realizing too late that something *really* bad must have happened.

Her tense expression and strained voice verified that. "When Laura was three months old…" She faltered.

Wil massaged her hand. "When our daughter was three months old, she was kidnapped."

Nick felt sick to his stomach. Although he had no children of his own, he did have nieces and nephews whom he loved, which gave him at least an inkling of what these two people must have suffered.

Samantha pulled herself together with an effort. "Naturally, we expected a ransom note. Have I mentioned that Wil was filthy rich, even then? Nevertheless, no note came." Her strong shoulders trembled with suppressed emotion.

Wil took up the tale. "Family and friends rallied around us, of course—Sam's sister, whose own little girl was just a few weeks younger than Laura. My brother, Peter—"

"The guy was a fruitcake," Samantha interrupted flatly.

Wil sighed. "I prefer to think of him as eccentric. You've got to admit, though, that in our darkest hour, he was a rock."

Samantha shrugged. "He didn't help so much as get in the way."

"The man's dead, Sam. We can afford to be charitable."

Nick nudged them back toward the point. "Did you ever get a ransom note?"

"No." Samantha's jaw clenched noticeably. "Months passed and the police didn't have a single lead that held up to investigation. That's when I decided we must call in a private eye. Wil disagreed. He expected the cops to come through."

"But you did it, anyway." Wil's hazel eyes darkened and he turned to Nick. "She hired Ray Jacobi. He'd been a captain in the Los Angeles Police Department, but quit to open a detective agency. When the strain on our marriage started to show, good old Ray was there to pick up the pieces."

"Don't be bitter, dear." It came out an angry purr. "If you'd hung around, maybe—"

"Hung around for what? Jacobi didn't come any closer to finding our child than the police had. All he found was you."

"*After* you gave up and moved to London."

"And *after* you went to work for him at his agency."

"Which was *after* our divorce. I was never unfaithful to you, Willy-boy. But I never gave up on Laura. *Never*. Not even when the police concluded she was probably dead." Samantha looked fierce as a lioness when she said it, her hands clenching into fists.

Wil Archer's hard expression changed to one of regret. "I know all that...now."

"So," Nick said, trying again to bring them back to the central issue, "Samantha became one of Jacobi's best operatives."

"Who says so?" she demanded. "I didn't."

Nick grinned. "*I* say so. I can't imagine you ever doing anything without becoming the best."

His ploy worked. She smiled. "Okay, you got my number."

"Then when your second husband died, you inherited and turned the business into the S. J. Spade Insurance Agency." A lightbulb went off. "I get it now. If you'd had a bodyguard for your child—"

Her groan interrupted his train of thought. "Don't say it. I can't bear to think that I let her down." She turned to Wil and he took her into his arms.

Nick watched them grieve together over a tragedy that was decades old. He'd never imagined his boss capable of such anguish. Stunned by her story, he felt relief that the man who shared her loss was there for her when she needed him.

But how had that happened? Surely coincidence was not involved here....

OUTSIDE THE OPEN WINDOW, Cory paused. She could hear the soft murmur of voices inside, followed by silence, so she knew Nick and Samantha were still up.

Reaching into the pocket of her jeans, she touched his money clip. Crystal had convinced her that she should return it to him tonight, since he'd said Samantha would be out late. Crystal's theory was that if Cory showed up on his doorstep with a ready-made excuse, he might decide to confide in her.

Only he obviously wasn't alone. She'd just have to creep silently away and not interrupt—

"Not a day goes by that I don't grieve for Laura. God, I must have been a lousy mother to let them take her! I don't care what the police think, I've always believed she was alive."

The anguish in Samantha's tone tore through Cory, halting her in her tracks.

A male voice she quickly identified as Wil Archer's responded. "You were a great mother, Sammy. It's not like she wandered away. She was stolen. How could we have anticipated that?"

"I suppose you're right, but still…"

I have to go, Cory scolded herself. *I shouldn't stand here shamelessly eavesdropping.* But instead of edging away, she edged closer, drawn by the raw emotion in the voice of that most self-controlled of women. "If I could only be sure she's not out there somewhere, needing me…."

"What can I do to help, Samantha?" That was Nick's voice, soft with compassion. "After all this time, what can anybody do?"

"Just having you here is a help, believe it or not—or a potential help, anyway. For a simple 'insurance' agent from San Francisco, you handle yourself real good."

"You should know. You own the agency."

Cory almost fainted from shock. Nick Charles was an insurance agent from California? Holy cow! They sure grew 'em different there.

Samantha went on. "Wil, can you pour me another one of your special martinis? Bitoa!"

"Bitoa?" Nick repeated.

Samantha's laughter sounded bitter. "*B-I-T-O-A*—booze is the only answer."

There was silence inside, then the shuffle of feet. Time for Cory to creep away, thoroughly ashamed of herself—and thoroughly glad to have learned at least a little about the mysterious Nick Charles and the glamorous Samantha Spade.

An insurance agent and a bereaved mother! Who'd have thought it?

WIL MADE A HELLUVA martini, Nick had to admit. He sipped it cautiously, then cleared his throat. "I think one of you was about to tell me what happened to bring you together here after all this time."

Wil and Samantha exchanged guarded glances. Then Samantha pulled a wad of paper from her pocket and handed it to Nick. He smoothed it out and read: "Greetings from Laura. If you go to Las Vegas and wait at La Paloma, you'll be getting warmer. Bring your checkbook."

"There have been others, too," Wil said. "'Laura wants to see you.' 'Laura needs your help.' 'Laura—'" His voice cracked.

Nick examined the note, written in pencil on cheap lined notebook paper. Looking at the uncertain nature of the script, he'd guess a right-handed person had written it left-handed. "You've both been getting these notes?" he asked.

"That's right."

"Postmarked where?"

"Las Vegas, Lake Tahoe, Carson City—from all over Nevada." Samantha finished her drink and set the stemmed glass on the table with a bang. The old spark leaped in her amber eyes. "Some asshole—pardon my French—some asshole obviously knows something about our missing child. We've got to find out who and what and…" She chewed on her lip for a moment before going on. "I've got to know if she's alive. Then, with a clear conscience, I can kill the guilty bastard who took her."

"Which is where I come in," Nick reminded her.

"Which is where you come in." She rose, tall and regal and tough as nails again. "You'll earn your money, sweetheart. Trust me on that."

He did. Watching her say good-night to Wil and send him on his way, watching her retreat into her bedroom, Nick was filled with an overwhelming admiration for Samantha Spade. Fate—or someone—had dealt her a bad hand, but she was playing it with the kind of bravado he could only admire. Wil wasn't a half-bad guy, either.

Nick thrust a hand into his trouser pocket and stiffened. He'd had a money clip in there with considerable cash when he and Cory left the casino.

He groaned. He'd been so busy groping the luscious Ms. Leblanc that he must have dropped the clip and never even noticed. Should he go over there now and—

No, he shouldn't. If he went, he'd stay, and that
would be a mistake.

Go to bed, Charles. It's only money.

CORY SAW NICK COMING and waved to attract his
attention. She'd been sitting at "their" umbrella
table beside the swimming pool for nearly an
hour already, drinking coffee and thinking about
what she'd overheard last night.

She was torn between shame at her flagrant
eavesdropping and disgust because she hadn't
stuck around to hear more. What she *had* heard
had kept her awake most of the night, anyway.

Samantha just didn't seem like the motherly
type, but maybe she had been, way back when-
ever. Obviously, she'd loved her child. After all
these years, she'd come to La Paloma to
find…closure, Cory supposed. And Samantha's
ex-husband, the father of her baby, had come to
help her.

Must be nice to have a man—to have *anyone*—
love you so much they'd travel halfway around
the world when you needed them. Now that her
parents were dead, Cory didn't have anyone except that elusive uncle.

Then there was the little matter of Nick's occu-
pation. What was it he'd said when she'd ques-
tioned him? Jack-of-all-trades, or something to
that effect. Now it turned out that he was just an
insurance agent traveling with his wealthy aunt,
owner of the agency where he worked.

Why hadn't he told her? Why was he being so
evasive about his profession? It was, after all, an
honorable one, even if far from exciting.

And then she knew the answer to her own question. She'd told him she was seeking adventure. What kind of adventure was she likely to find with an insurance agent? He was merely trying to help her dream along. What difference would such an innocent deception make, anyway, when they'd soon be going their separate ways, never to meet again?

That inevitability made her stomach clench. She liked Nick a lot—really, *really* liked Nick. She liked him so much she was determined to lure him into her bed even it if turned out to be a one-night stand. She shuddered at the thought. As Crystal always said with a wink, "Better to have loved and lost than never to have—"

Not *love*, Cory corrected: *like*. She didn't know him well enough to feel anything more than animal attraction. *But,* a little voice complained in her ear, *you know Roger really well but you sure don't love him. You wouldn't love him if he were the last man on earth.*

She groaned into her coffee cup. When had life gotten so complicated?

And here Nick was now, the man with whom she'd discovered "like at first sight," leaning down to drop a kiss on the top of her head. A kiss he held for a long moment, then punctuated with a sigh.

"Your hair smells good, like desert flowers." He broke contact to pull out a chair and slump into it. He smiled, but he looked tired and troubled. "You didn't happen to find my money clip last night, did you?"

In response, she pulled the clip loaded with

bills from her hot pink tote and passed it to him. He stuffed it into his shorts pocket without counting the money. "Thanks."

"You're welcome." She cocked her head, examining his face. He seemed tense and distracted. "Are you all right?"

He nodded, first to her and then to the waiter who'd appeared with a fresh cup and a carafe of coffee. He waited until the waiter had withdrawn before responding. Then he said, "I'm fine. It's Samantha I'm worried about."

"Oh?" How curious and uninvolved Cory sounded; how guilty she *was*.

He sipped his coffee. "She...suffered a terrible loss a number of years ago. Now it seems as if out of nowhere, all kinds of things are happening to remind her of it."

"Is there anything I can do for you or Samantha?" Cory ventured.

"For Samantha, not a thing. For me...I can always use a friend."

Friend? That wasn't nearly enough. "I can do better than that," she said rashly. "Come to my place and I'll..." she licked her lips "...help you relax." Lord, she couldn't believe she'd said that—or that she could meet his gaze so boldly, promising all kinds of earthly delights she wasn't sure she could deliver.

He held that gaze until it sizzled between them. Then he stood up abruptly. "Why the hell not?" he exclaimed. "We've been tap-dancing around it ever since we met and time's running out."

He offered his hand. She took it and let him pull her to her feet, her movements slow and languid, as if she were moving underwater. The intensity of his gaze practically paralyzed her.

"Grab your bag and let's get out of here," he said. "If we're going to do this—"

"Nick, there you are."

He stiffened, turning toward the voice. Joel Caspar, dapper in white trousers and a pale blue polo shirt, hurried up.

"It's Sammy," he said. "I think something's wrong. Something about Laura—"

"Not here!" Nick's tone of command cut off the man's words. "Talk to the lady, not to me."

"But she said you're her insurance, so—"

"Damn it, man, not now! Find Samantha. She's around here somewhere with Wil Archer." Nick grabbed Cory's hand and hauled her after him.

"But—"

"But, nothing." Dragging Cory at a half run around a corner, Nick muttered, "Now that we've made up our minds, let's get out of here before—"

"Nicholas! Hold up!"

At Samantha's command, Cory slowed, hauling back on Nick's hand. "It's your aunt," she said, chastising him. "You've got to see what she wants."

"Do I have to?" He looked like a petulant little boy.

He also looked sexy as hell, ready to give her all the romance she could handle and then some. But she must be strong. "You have to," she said firmly.

Samantha and Wil steamed up. Samantha nodded to Cory. "Hello, Miss Leblanc. You're looking well."

"So are you." It was the absolute truth. Samantha wore full and flowing navy blue slacks with a soft white silk shirt. A broad red leather belt cinched her narrow waist. Cory resisted the urge to look around for the camera crew, this woman looked so perfectly turned out.

Nick shuffled his feet impatiently. "Whatta ya want, Sammy?"

She gave him a narrow glance. "A little respect, for starters. No one calls me Sammy unless they've known me for many years."

Cory blinked in surprise. "Who'd know you longer than your nephew?"

"My nephew?" The woman glanced at Nick and burst out laughing. "Nephew, dearest, stop glaring at me. There have been many times I didn't want to claim you."

"Ha-ha, very funny."

"I'll rephrase," she said. "Only those who have known me for many years—and childhood doesn't count."

"Got it, Auntie Samantha. So what do you want from me?"

"Why…" She looked downright ingenious. "The pleasure of your company for cocktails later. Say eight o'clock in the bungalow? You, too, Miss Leblanc," she added as if in an afterthought.

"Please call me Cory."

"Certainly. And you may call me Ms. Spade."

Nick scowled. "We'll consider your invitation. Anything else?"

"Not a thing, dear boy. Run along and enjoy

yourselves doing whatever it is you're both so hot to do."

"She knows," Cory hissed, trotting along behind Nick. "How embarrassing."

"Embarrassing enough to call the whole thing off?"

"Oh, Nick!" She hugged his arm, which was all she had access to. "Of course not. I was thinking of you."

"Don't." He slid an arm around her waist without slackening his pace. "Think of yourself—always. Now let's *go* before someone else shows up."

ONCE INSIDE HER BUNGALOW, Cory was overwhelmed by nerves. She didn't know what to say or do, so she just turned toward him, hoping to take her cues from him.

In the drowsy half light, he looked at her with hooded eyes, but made no move to touch her. "It's your party," he said softly. "What games shall we play?"

She shivered. Games. She'd never played *games*, not the kind he meant. "Well," she said nervously, "you could be Tarzan and I could be Jane. Or you could be Robin Hood and I'll be Maid Marian. Or—"

"Or I could be Nick and you could be Cory and we could just let nature take its course." He reached up, unbuttoned his polo shirt and whipped it over his head in one smooth yank. "Do you have any idea how hard it's been for me *not* to carry you off and make mad passionate love to you?"

She stared at him, wide-eyed. "Really? I had no idea." Dry mouthed, she licked her lips, considering her next move. Deciding it was time to put up or shut up, she fumbled at the hem of her gauzy blouse, then slid it over her head with as much aplomb as she could muster.

Now it was his turn to stare.

Her breasts might as well have been naked; the sheer wisp of bra concealed nothing. She could feel her nipples puckering in response to his attention.

He kicked off his leather sandals, challenging her.

She matched him with her white leather flats, lifting her chin triumphantly. So far so good. Never in her wildest flights of fancy had she ever imagined undressing like this in front of a man. But now she was halfway there and she hadn't fainted with embarrassment, so she could probably make it all the way.

Crystal would be proud!

Slowly, holding her gaze, he unbuckled his belt and pulled it through the loops of his khaki trousers. Tossing it aside, he unbuttoned his waistband and pulled the zipper down.

"Oh, stop!" She bit her lip, horrified that she'd been unable to take the pressure. He responded immediately by pulling the zipper back up. "I mean, don't stop," she amended, feeling her cheeks flame. "I mean..." Desperately she fumbled for a way out. "Couldn't I just close my eyes and let you s-surprise me?"

For the longest moment, he simply looked confused. Then he grinned. "As I said before, it's your party. You want a surprise, I'll give you a surprise."

Stepping forward, he put his hands on her elbows and guided her backward until she came up against the foot of the bed. She was so rigid that it took some urging on his part before she unbent enough to sit down.

He fondled her breasts through the sheer nothing and she gasped. "Close your eyes," he whispered. "Leave everything to me."

She moaned. "Are you sure?"

"Aren't you?"

She closed her eyes. In the velvety blackness, she heard the rustle of fabric hitting the floor, a soft footstep. In her mind's eye, she could see him in all his naked glory. She bit her lip to keep from groaning, then tried to concentrate on remembering to breathe.

Nothing happened.

"Are you there?" she asked in alarm. Was she sitting all alone in this room, half-naked on her bed?

"Shh." His breath stirred the tendrils of hair near her ear. He fumbled for a moment at the clasp holding her bra in place; she felt the sudden easing of pressure and then he guided the straps from her arms. "Stand up," he commanded in a voice that lulled while it excited.

"I'm...not sure I can."

"Try."

Hands on her waist lifted her, peeled everything away. She stood there with her eyes pressed shut, feeling dizzy and disoriented and sexier than she'd ever felt in her life. "Now what?" she murmured.

"Whatever you like."

She considered for a moment. Then she lifted her arms high and fell backward onto the bed. A wonderful feeling of freedom and joy filled her.

This was insane. This *wasn't* Corinne Leblanc, it was her twin—not her *evil* twin, her *brave* twin. She opened her eyes and smiled.

"Come to Mama," she said.

He didn't have to be asked twice.

THEY LAY ON THE KING-SIZE bed side by side, their bodies not quite touching yet. Ah, but their hands...stroking, exploring, curious and eager. Lifting his head, he pressed his mouth to hers and slowly, deliberately, coaxed apart lips that needed no coaxing. The kiss was long...languid...possessive.

Cory could hardly breathe. Her skin felt alive, excitement running through her in concert with his touch. Her breasts ached for it. With incredible daring, she cupped his lean cheeks with her hands and directed his mouth to her nipple. He nuzzled the stiff peak, flicked it with his tongue, finally drew it deep into the hot wet interior of his mouth. This elicited a strangled moan from her arched throat.

Her hands, braver than she was, found his erection. Stroking and lifting, she squirmed while he suckled at first one nipple and then the other. Her entire body filled with tingling pleasure and she found herself drifting into a gentle, erotic self-absorption unlike anything she'd ever known before.

He left her breasts and his head dipped lower, his tongue tickling her navel. She caught her breath, but he wasn't stopping there. With one hand, he explored the inner contours of her trembling thighs. With the other hand he cupped the mound of curls at the joining, sliding his fingers back and forth until, with a sigh, she let him spread her legs apart.

His probing finger hesitated, slid smoothly inside. The flush of pleasure spiraled through her, magnified when a second finger joined the first. She writhed, opening to him completely. He heightened her pleasure still more by biting her nipples just hard enough to add another level of delight.

Her head whirled and she drifted, giddy and weightless. For a few minutes he played with her, taking her to the very edge. She fought back, unwilling to let go, determined to savor these sensations fully before giving in to the tempest gathering inside.

His mouth touched her *there* and she stiffened with shock, her thighs automatically tightening. Undeterred, he sought entrance with his tongue, and that's when she lost it in a way she never had before, coming apart in spasms that left her weak and shaking.

He raised above her on his hands and knees, his face dark and intense. Still quivering in the aftermath, she looked at him helplessly, doubting that she could satisfy him now.

He didn't look worried. Settling himself between her thighs, he pushed in slowly with a smooth, strong stroke that told her how wrong she'd been to think she had nothing left. As he started to move with steady precision, she found herself responding with fierce pleasure.

And then it happened, the climax she'd never quite reached before—almost like those few seconds of weightlessness at the apex of a dive, only better...and longer. And when it was over, she knew that she would never, ever get enough of this man.

Especially not in the lousy three days they had left.

6

FOR LONG SWEET MOMENTS, he lay like a deadweight on her satisfied body. When he started to roll away, she uttered a protest and wrapped her arms around him fiercely.

"I'm too heavy," he objected. "I'll crush you." But he stopped trying to move.

"If you do, I'll die smiling." She kissed his cheek, and she was indeed smiling.

"You've got a point." Repressed laughter laced his tone. "But as much as I'm enjoying this, I won't be able to relax until I'm sure you're still breathing. I've got plans for you, my girl."

Distracted by thoughts of what those plans might be, she let him slide to one side, where he settled snugly against her. They smiled at each other, silly contented smiles.

She sighed luxuriously. "I feel so good, it kind of makes me wonder why we wasted so much time."

"That's my line." He began to toy with her nipple, tweaking and tugging while the most delicious sensations swept through her exhausted but not quite comatose body. "You've still got a couple of days." Leaning over, he dropped a kiss just below her left nipple. "What's that?"

She felt the tentative touch of his tongue. "A

birthmark, I guess. I've always had it.'' She squirmed happily beneath his attention, her breathing quickening. ''How much longer will you be staying at La Paloma?''

He covered her breast with his hand and squeezed gently. ''I'm not sure. Whatever Samantha decides.''

''Samantha.''

He gave her a quizzical look. ''I know you don't like her—''

''I never said that.'' Cory might have felt it, but she'd never said it.

He slid his hand from her breast to her rib cage, then past her waist to linger on her stomach. ''You didn't have to say it.''

''Maybe, but that was before—'' She bit off the words. She wasn't supposed to know about Samantha's lost baby, so there was no way she could explain her change of heart. Nor could she tip him off that she knew he was an insurance agent working for his aunt. Why they'd want to keep such a benign secret, she couldn't imagine. As long as they did, though, she'd have to watch every word around him...unless he decided to come clean himself. She licked her lips, finding it hard to concentrate when he was doing such delightful things to her.

His clever hand explored lower. ''That was before what?''

''Before...before...'' She dragged in a deep, quivering breath. ''Oh, Nick, how can I give you a coherent answer when you're...doing things like...*that?*''

''Like this?''

Every little movement had a meaning all its own. She groaned and began to move against his hand, touching his arms with her fingertips, savoring the feel of warm hard satin. "You're... really good at this," she said in a choked voice.

"Thank you." His reply was muted by the nipple he'd begun teasing with his tongue. "You're not half-bad yourself."

She took that as validation of her own participation, a validation desperately needed. "I'm one of those people who get better with practice," she gasped. "Maybe if you just quit worrying about crushing me—"

"I've got a better idea."

His hands closed around her waist and he lifted her spraddle-legged across his hips. Enthralled and half-dazed, she saw the strain on his face as he lowered her with exquisite slowness, parting her, pressing her down, penetrating until they were completely joined. Once he had her firmly in place, he moved his hands to her breasts, drawing them down to meet his seeking mouth.

She had never felt so sexy or so womanly. Her head swam and her heart soared with ever swirling movement. His hands left her breasts and slid down to grab her hips, setting a new rhythm. Reeling from a multitude of physical reactions, she placed her palms on his strong chest for balance, then stroked the flat nipples pricking her palms.

He reacted instantly, his harsh groan confirming his rising excitement. He stroked his hands down to her bottom, increasing the speed and power of their joining. It was more than she could stand. An orgasm rushed over her with a speed and intensity that tore a strangled cry of fulfillment from her throat.

She wanted it to go on forever. As he hurtled toward his own release, she held him tight and wondered frantically if there might be some way…any way…to make these next few days last forever.

"COME BACK WITH ME for cocktail hour and then I'll take you to dinner."

Sitting on the edge of the bed in a light summer robe, with her hair a tangle and her body tingling from several long, lovely bouts of lovemaking, Cory sighed. "Do you think that's a good idea? I've softened toward Samantha, I really have, but *she* doesn't like me one little bit."

"*I* like you."

He'd pulled on his trousers, but hadn't zipped or buttoned them yet. Seeing him standing there all tousled and half-naked, Cory wanted to throw off her clothes and start over again.

She smiled at the thought. "I like you, too," she said sincerely. "But as far as Samantha is concerned…"

"She has her reasons, Cory. She's a complicated woman." He spoke slowly, obviously choosing his words with care. "Even people who don't like her—and there are more than a few of them out there—find all those complications strangely fascinating."

"I find her rude, basically. And bossy."

"That's on the outside. She has hidden depths." He cocked his head, looking thoughtful. "She doesn't let many people get close to her," he said finally. "Once they do, though, they're almost fanatically loyal."

"Sorry, I just don't get it. Maybe if I knew a little more about her…"

He shook his head. "No can do. That would have to come from her."

"Then tell me about *you*. Now that we've become…" she glanced significantly at the bed "…intimate, I think I deserve to know at least a little about the mysterious Nick Charles."

His eyes widened in mock surprise. "Me, mysterious? I'm just a simple lad from—*out there*." He made a sweeping gesture with one strong, tanned arm. "I've never thought it was important where a person's from. It's where they're going that matters."

"I'll bite. Where *are* you going?"

He grinned. "Back to the bungalow to have drinks with Samantha. Come with me. Maybe she can be prevailed upon to satisfy at least a little of your curiosity."

"I don't know…."

"You were invited, Cory."

"I don't think she meant it."

For a moment, he looked ready to argue. Then he shrugged and buttoned his trousers. "Suit yourself. I'm just surprised you'd let her intimidate you."

He'd said that deliberately, she knew he had, but still it brought her shoulders back and her chin up. Nobody and nothing scared her off.

Well, nobody and nothing, now that her parents were both dead. While they lived, the mere thought of disappointing them had intimidated her plenty.

"Do you mind waiting while I pull myself together?" she inquired sweetly.

"Not in the slightest. In fact—" the trousers came off a lot faster than they'd gone on "—I'll help."

The shower took considerably longer than expected.

SAMANTHA DID NOT LOOK pleased to see them. One corner of her scarlet mouth curled up in something akin to a grimace. Her sharp glance flicked over Cory and then returned to Nick. "Nice of you to drop by," she said ungraciously.

"We were invited." Nick took Cory's elbow and steered her past their prickly hostess. "You mentioned drinks, as I recall."

"That's right—drinks. At eight o'clock. It's now after nine."

"I've been busy."

"I do believe you have." Samantha 's eyes narrowed and she gave them a rather pointed glance. "Are the two of you an item?"

Nick grinned. "As the saying goes, we're just good friends."

"Better friends than you were a few hours ago, unless I miss my guess."

Cory's face flamed, embarrassment written all over it. Annoyed with Samantha for putting her on the defensive, Nick decided to take the conversational bull by the horns. "Since you've guessed our little secret, you should understand why I'd like to tell Cory a little more about the reasons behind our trip here," he said. "She's been a bit put off by—"

"No."

"Now, Samantha—"

"Clam up, Nicky." She nodded abruptly toward the bar cart. "How are you on martinis?"

"Lousy. I'll give it a shot only under duress." He glanced at Cory, who gave him a helpless shrug. She looked great in hot pink and purple silk that rippled over her body, touching here, touching there, suggesting a lot and revealing little.

That glance brought back memories of a helluva shower. It made his mouth water to think of her backed up against that shower stall with her legs wrapped around him and her arms grabbing for him and her—

He cleared his throat. "Cory, what would you like, and don't get fancy on me."

"A vodka and tonic would be fine," she murmured.

He rummaged through the bottles on the cart. "We've got vodka and tonic, but we're out of gin, Samantha."

"Oh, for the love of Pete."

She stomped over to see for herself, the fullness of her flowered silk pants swinging around her legs. She'd tied up the matching silk blouse to expose her midriff, something she seemed to enjoy doing. Of course, as nice as her midriff was, he could understand her affection for showing it. Go with your strength, his old pappy used to say. She

WELCOME TO THE
CASINO!

Try your luck at the Roulette Wheel ...
Play a hand of Twenty-One!

How to play:

1. Play the Roulette and Twenty-One scratch-off games, as instructed on the

opposite page, to see that you are eligible for FREE BOOKS and a FREE GIFT!

2. Send back the card and you'll receive TWO brand-new Harlequin Temptation® novels. These books have a cover price of $3.75 each, but they are yours to keep absolutely free.

3. There's no catch. You're under no obligation to buy anything. We charge nothing — ZERO — for your first shipment. And you don't have to make any minimum number of purchases — not even one!

4. The fact is, thousands of readers enjoy receiving books by mail from the Harlequin Reader Service® before they're available in stores. They like the convenience of home delivery, and they love our discount prices!

5. We hope that after receiving your free books you'll want to remain a subscriber. But the choice is yours — to continue or cancel, any time at all!

So why not take us up on our invitation, with no risk of any kind. You'll be glad you did!

Play Twenty-One For This Exquisite Free Gift!

THIS SURPRISE
MYSTERY GIFT
COULD BE
YOURS FREE WHEN
YOU PLAY
TWENTY-ONE

It's fun, and we're giving away **FREE GIFTS** to all players!

PLAY ROULETTE!

Scratch the silver to see where the ball has landed—7 RED or 11 BLACK makes you eligible for TWO FREE romance novels!

PLAY TWENTY-ONE!

Scratch the silver to reveal a winning hand! Congratulations, you have Twenty-One. Return this card promptly and you'll receive a fabulous free mystery gift, along with your free books!

YES!

Please send me all the free Harlequin Temptation® books and the gift for which I qualify! I understand that I am under no obligation to purchase any books, as explained on the back of this card.

Name (please print clearly)

Address   Apt.#

City   State   Zip

The Harlequin Reader Service® — Here's how it works:

Accepting free books places you under no obligation to buy anything. You may keep the books and gift and return the shipping statement marked "cancel." If you do not cancel, about a month later we'll send you 4 additional novels and bill you just $3.12 each, plus 25¢ delivery per book and applicable sales tax, if any.* That's the complete price — and compared to cover prices of $3.75 each — quite a bargain! You may cancel at any time, but if you choose to continue, every month we'll send you 4 more books, which you may either purchase at the discount price...or return to us and cancel your subscription.

*Terms and prices subject to change without notice. Sales tax applicable in N.Y.

wore the usual spike-heeled, ankle-strapped sandals.

Realizing he'd told her the truth about the liquor supply, she turned away with a grimace. "I suppose I could handle a vodka and tonic, if I must," she grumbled, her tone making it clear that she was doing this under protest. "Then again, maybe Wil has gin. I'll call him."

"Sorry, love." Wil stood in the open doorway, wearing a white suit and baby blue shirt. He looked like a very proper gentleman touring the tropics. "I'm already here and I don't have a drop of gin. Make that four vodka and tonics, Nick." He smiled and nodded to include Cory. "Ms. Leblanc. Glad you could join us."

"The tonic's flat," Nick said.

Samantha made an annoyed hissing sound. "This is getting ridiculous. I'll call Joel and have him—"

"Calm down, my love." Wil patted her shoulder. "I saw a liquor deliveryman outside on my way here. Perhaps he'll have something that will save the day."

"If I don't have a drink in my hand in the next five minutes, there'll be no day left to save." She spoke through gritted teeth.

Wil departed. Samantha paced. Nick and Cory exchanged significant glances. Finally he said, "Did something happen today, Samantha?"

"Like what?" she snapped.

"I don't know. You're so touchy that I thought maybe…"

Standing before an open window, she jerked

her head around to glare at him. "Stop thinking, Nick. You're not good at it."

"That's not what you said when you told me I was coming along on this gig."

"Clam up." She glanced at Cory significantly, then turned back to the window. After a moment, she swiveled around again, her face more composed. "You'll forgive my impatience, of course." She actually managed to both look and sound as if she meant it as an apology. "I'll admit I'm edgy tonight. I have a feeling—"

"No gin," Wil announced from the door, "but I've got a nearly full bottle of guaranteed fresh tonic here. That should hold us while the waiter fetches a proper supply."

"Thank God," Samantha muttered.

Nick had the feeling her miniprayer covered considerably more than simply a well-stocked bar.

THE TENSION IN THE ROOM was palpable.

Cory sipped her drink slowly and tried not to think about anything except the moment. Certainly she didn't want to remember the hours she'd spent in her bungalow with the man now sitting so sedately at her side. If she did, she'd lose her concentration entirely.

You needed concentration around Samantha.

Admittedly, Cory didn't know the other woman very well; she wondered if anyone did. Even upon such slight, and at times acrimonious, acquaintance, it was obvious to Cory that tonight Samantha was nervous as a cat in a roomful of rocking chairs. Her usual staccato manner of

speaking was actually intensified, and she kept
leaping from her chair to pace to the window and
back. The faint fragrance of gardenia followed
her.

Finally even Wil, who appeared to worship the
ground his ex-wife walked on, spoke up. "Ye
gods, Sammy. All that pacing is making *me* nervous."

"It's not doing a whole helluva lot for me, either," she snapped. "Guess we'll both just have to
live with it."

He took no offense. "Won't you tell me what's
bothering you, love? Are you keeping something
from me?"

Cory felt Nick grow still and watchful, as if he
had no more insight than she into the restless
mind of this woman. She gave him a curious
glance, but intent upon his aunt, he didn't seem to
notice.

Samantha clenched her teeth on a groan. "It's a
feeling, that's all."

"A feeling of...?"

"Who the hell knows? Doom!" She looked at
her empty glass. "Somebody want to fix me another one of these things? Where's that guy with
the gin?"

"He'll be here." Wil took her glass and crossed
to the bar cart.

Samantha sat down in the chair he'd vacated.
She looked straight at Cory, who until this point
had managed to stay in the background. "So," Samantha said, "when are you flying home to Ar-
kansas, Corinne?"

"In three days—and it's Texas." Cory clenched

her hand around the strap of her small evening bag, thinking she'd like to sling it in Samantha's face. She'd asked the woman any number of times to call her Cory.

"I was in Texas once." Samantha slumped elegantly in her chair. "I found it to be big and dusty and full of hot air."

"It's not alone in that distinction," Cory retorted, "so far as the hot air goes, at any rate." Suddenly she lifted her hand to her mouth to cover a prodigious yawn. "Excuse me! I'm suddenly so sleepy."

"Or bored." Samantha also covered a yawn. "Now you've got me doing it. Yawns are contagious, you know."

Cory was having trouble keeping her eyes open. When she turned her head to look at Nick, he was frowning at her with a perplexed expression. She tried to reach out, to touch his hand, but couldn't quite lift her arm.

She attempted a smile that never quite cracked the stiff plane of her lips. Her mouth was growing dry and fuzzy. "What did you put in that drink?" she asked, meaning it as a joke, but realizing it didn't sound that way. "I've never had alcohol hit me so fast."

Wil shrugged, an eyebrow climbing. "It's the fresh tonic," he said, his eyes twinkling. "One must watch those mixes."

"That's a theory I never..." Another yawn. Cory felt herself disintegrating before their very eyes. Despite the humiliation, there didn't seem to be much she could do about it.

Samantha gave Wil a significant glance. "She's tired because she spent the day getting—"

"If you say 'laid,'" Nick interrupted, his tone deadly serious, "you're a dead woman."

"*Moi?*" Her voice radiated astonished innocence. "I was about to say 'better acquainted with my handsome nephew.'"

Cory couldn't keep her eyes open one second longer. Although she could still hear them chatting casually, she was sinking deeper and deeper into sleep. She felt Nick slide an arm around her shoulders and pull her over to nestle against him, heard Wil say, "Poor thing, she's positively exhausted. *Is* this your doing, Nicholas?" and then Samantha's sly laughter, followed by another prodigious yawn.

Then Cory heard nothing at all.

NICK OPENED EYES that felt like sheets of sandpaper rubbing together. He saw nothing but darkness. A weight lay across his chest, and a pounding ache threatened to blow the lid off his head at any moment.

Where was he? What had happened?

Was he alive or dead?

The weight holding him pinned in place shifted and a hand brushed across his mouth. He heard a groan and realized that was no weight, that was a woman—and unless he missed his guess, a woman named Cory.

He didn't know how long he lay there trying to get his bearings. With time his vision cleared and he saw moonlight streaming through the window

to illuminate the bamboo furniture of the bungalow where he'd been having drinks with...

Damn!

"Samantha?" He called her name softly in the
velvet darkness, but heard nothing except his
pounding heart. "Wil?"

He tried again, louder this time. Again, silence
greeted him.

Adrenaline shot through his system. Something was very, very wrong here. Carefully he
eased himself out from beneath Cory's limp body.
Leaving her crumpled on the settee, he stumbled
for the floor lamp behind the chair. Illumination
flooded the room.

In an equally strong flash, understanding hit
him.

Somebody had slipped them a Mickey in that
bottle of tonic. Now here he stood with a split
skull, his paramour comatose, his boss and her ex
missing in action. *Some bodyguard.*

Stumbling to the bathroom, he threw cold water on his face and swore himself into full awareness. Returning to the sitting room, he looked
around with bloodshot eyes. The glasses they'd
been drinking from lay on the floor at various an-
gles, just as they'd been dropped.

It took only another moment to spot what he
was looking for, there on the table in plain sight: a
sheet of lined notebook paper, the kind kids used,
with a penciled message.

"Sit tight and keep your trap shut if you ever
want to see Sammy and Wilmer again. No cops or
they're buzzard bait. Wait for orders and don't
get cute."

Wilmer? Archer's first name was *Wilmer?*

Nick swore terribly. Cory groaned and thrashed about on the small settee, but didn't open her eyes.

What did she have to do with all this?

Nothing, of course, and yet…

He was looking at everything and everyone with suspicion, but how could he not? While he'd been concentrating on Cory, someone else had been concentrating on Samantha.

Was his initial meeting with Cory in the lobby really an accident or had it been planned?

You're crazy, Charles, he berated himself—but hadn't Samantha guessed that Cory didn't really have an Uncle Mario? Thrusting his hands through his hair, Nick tried to think. Surely Cory was exactly what she seemed: a very nice, very naive, very sexy woman.

Or was she? Maybe she was actually a plant to keep him from doing his job properly. Maybe she knew more about this cockamamie caper than he did.

But she'd been first to succumb to the drug, whatever it was. At the time, he'd thought, in an admittedly maudlin way, that it was a tribute to his prowess; he really *had* worn her out. That's what everyone thought. They'd smiled at her and shook their heads knowingly and…keeled over in turn.

Why had Cory decided upon today of all days to take him to her bed? Why not yesterday or tomorrow?

Because, he answered himself, today was the day her confederates chose to snatch Samantha and Wil. For some reason, they'd been unable to pull it off while Nick and Cory were otherwise occupied, so they'd settled on plan B—a round of Mickeys.

Leaning down, he lifted Cory's eyelid and saw nothing but white. If she wasn't out, she sure as hell gave a good impression of it. He should shake her awake and then shake the truth out of her. Even as he thought it, his hands closed over her shoulders in a crushing grip.

He stopped himself just in time.

What would that gain him? If she knew he was on to her, he'd never get anything useful out of her. He had to be smarter than that. He mustn't let her know he realized that he'd been set up.

He felt stronger now, physically as well as mentally. Whatever they'd given him was wearing off and it'd be wearing off for Cory soon, too. When it did, he had to be ready.

Leaning over, he rolled her into his arms and stood up, holding her against his chest. For a moment he was struck anew by the soft sweet weight of her, the smell of flowers he'd come to associate with her hair, the clear brow and the delicious lips.

But he wouldn't be played for a sap twice by the same woman. If she was mixed up in this— and he was reluctantly coming to that conclusion—she'd pay for it.

Big time.

Laura was somehow the key, he realized. Her name had been invoked to get her still-grieving parents here, and keep them here. If he could discover what had happened to Laura—

All the air burst from his lungs and he nearly dropped the woman in his arms.

Could he be holding Laura?

7

CORY WOKE UP IN STAGES, each stage more miserable than the one before it. First she became aware that her eyes were glued shut; at least, she didn't seem able to open them. Then the horrible dryness of her mouth registered, followed by a penetrating pain that started at one temple and lanced straight to the other.

She groaned, not knowing where she was or what had happened to her and afraid that when she found out—

"Waking up, Sleeping Beauty?"

Nick's voice, thank God. She wasn't drifting alone in some alternate reality, after all. She tried to say his name and found she couldn't.

She felt the touch of his lips on her throbbing temple and imagined that the pain immediately lessened.

"Head hurt?" he inquired. "Maybe this will help."

She mourned the loss of his lips, but the cold damp cloth that replaced them, covering her temples and her eyes, was a blessing. "What happened?" she managed to croak.

"First have a drink of water."

He cradled her head and lifted it tenderly. The

rim of a glass bumped her teeth and she drank blindly. The water felt and tasted heavenly.

"So what happened?" she asked again, more strongly this time. Lifting a corner of the wet cloth, she managed to pry open one eye. Her vision was so blurry she could barely make him out, but one thing was obvious: they were in bed together. Groaning, she lowered the cloth again.

His soft chuckle was not reassuring. "You drank too much and passed out," he said. "I carried you back here to put you to bed. You remember waking up, right? It was your idea for me to stay."

She could well believe that. The part she had trouble with was his casual declaration that she'd passed out. "I only had one drink," she protested. "How could I—"

"One drink? Maybe that's all you *recall*, but you had considerably more than that."

"I...don't remember any more," she admitted. "I hope I didn't—you know—make a fool of myself or anything."

"You were fine." He stroked her cheek and she luxuriated in his healing touch. "I'm just relieved that Samantha finally answered your questions. Now we won't have that between us, messing up what time we have left."

Attempted concentration sent another pain shooting through her head. "Samantha answered my questions?"

After a moment's silence, he said, "Don't tell me you've forgotten, after you made such a fuss about it."

"I haven't forgotten. I...don't remember in the

first place." She chewed on her lower lip, feeling faintly queasy. "I'm sorry, Nick. I don't know what's wrong with me, but I have no memory at all beyond that first drink."

He stretched out beside her and the mattress shifted beneath his weight. The touch of his hand on her throat warmed her, soothed her.

"Poor baby," he murmured. "I had no idea—but we'll skip that. Okay, what Samantha told you, in a nutshell, was that I'm the black sheep of the family—kind of a playboy, if you want to know exactly what she said. I'm a Hollywood casting director, actually, but I don't advertise the fact because there are wannabe actors beneath every rock."

"A casting director?" That didn't ring true, but at the moment Cory couldn't dredge up any reason why not. He *had* seemed on intimate terms with that actress.

"Samantha's a wealthy, twice-divorced widow, as you already knew," he continued. "Her life, if you ask me, is pretty much meaningless. She travels, always with a member of the family in tow because she distrusts strangers. This just happened to be my turn to accommodate her. Since she always picks up the tab, how could I refuse?"

"Is she also from southern California?"

"That's right. She has a place in La Jolla."

Cory knew that wasn't true. She didn't know how she knew, but maybe it would come to her if she survived. For the moment, she simply sighed. "She must think I'm an idiot."

"Not a chance. She was distracted herself, since

she and Wil were getting ready to take a private little trip to Lake Tahoe."

Cory finally found the strength to pull the cloth from her eyes so she could really see him. "They're leaving?"

"They've left. You said goodbye and wished them bon voyage."

His mouth smiled but his eyes didn't. Or maybe her eyes weren't capable of seeing what was actually in his. "At least I showed good manners," she said dispiritedly.

"That you did." He kissed her eyes closed. "I'm glad they're gone. It'll give me more time to concentrate on you. Go back to sleep now, baby. You'll feel better after a little rest."

"Will you be here when I wake up?"

"Just try to shake me."

He didn't need to sound so grim, she thought drowsily. She settled against him with a sigh. *So Samantha told me everything*, she thought as she drifted off again, *and all of it was lies....*

HE WAS THERE when she woke up, all right, but he was *not* concentrating on her. At first she thought he might be annoyed with her for passing out the way she had, but when she mentioned it he simply stared at her as if she'd gone mad and told her she was imagining things.

Like she'd imagined hearing Samantha talk about her kidnapped child? And hearing—make that overhearing—that Samantha owned an insurance agency in San Francisco where Nick was employed?

None of it made sense to Cory, but she couldn't

see any sinister reasons for the discrepancies. When she thought about it logically, she supposed Samantha had simply made up a story, for whatever reason, and forced Nick to stick to it. What was it Cory's father used to say when he was teasing her?

"I'll lie and you swear to it."

That was the kind of relationship Samantha and Nick had, all right. Anything she said seemed all right with him.

Had Samantha told him not to make love to Cory again? Because he didn't—not for two days and two nights. He never strayed far from her side, and he was attentive, but he did *not* take her to bed for purposes other than sleeping.

During the day, he spent most of his time on the telephone, although she had no idea who he was speaking to or why. She did think he was beginning to look a bit tense and preoccupied, however.

Her vacation definitely wasn't ending up the way she'd hoped. She hadn't even *seen* her uncle, but that didn't seem so important once she'd met and bedded the intriguing Nicholas Charles. The *missing* Nicholas Charles, actually. Here she was, set to fly back to Houston tomorrow afternoon, and Nick had taken off for Las Vegas on business without her. Worse, he wasn't sure when he'd return and had told her to go to dinner without him.

Not a happy camper, Cory Leblanc picked up the telephone and dialed Crystal, who would certainly think of *something* that could be done.

NICK CHARLES WASN'T a happy camper, either.

In two days, he'd turned up nothing: two days of searching his bungalow and Cory's, two days of calling in every favor he'd ever done, two days of waiting for a ransom note or an extortion note or a suicide note.

He had even called the S. J. Spade Insurance Agency to speak to Mark Spenser, Samantha's liaison.

"I need some information and I need it fast," Nick had said. "First, I want the birth certificate of Corinne Leblanc of Houston, Texas—father Andre, mother Rhea Moretti Leblanc. Then I want—"

"You have authorization for all this, of course."

Nick counted to ten. Then he counted to ten again. "Look, Spenser," he finally growled, "this is life or death. Get me?"

"Let me speak to the boss."

"If I had access to the boss, *she'd* be calling you instead of me." Nick let that sink in with an ominous silence. "Now are you going to get on this or do I have to—"

"No, no, I'll take care of it." The guy sounded shaken. "What else do you need?"

"The birth certificate, and death certificate if there is one, for Laura Archer, parents Samantha and Wilmer—"

"Oh, my God!" Mark's voice trembled with shock. "You don't mean…?"

"Actually, I do. And this is confidential, got it? I want all those certificates compared to a set of fingerprints I'm overnighting to you."

"Yes, of course. It won't be easy but—"

"I don't want it easy, I want it *now*. Call in every favor Samantha ever did, but get the job done. And Mark? If you can't reach me when you need me, Joel Caspar here at La Paloma will cover for me. Get it?"

"Got it."

"Good."

But before he'd had a chance to contact Joel, Nick got a half-hysterical telephone call from the man and realized he had to act fast. Making lemonade out of lemons, he decided to give Cory enough rope to hang herself by telling her he'd been called to Las Vegas for a business meeting that might stretch into the wee hours. If she thought he was completely out of the picture, she might make a mistake.

He could only hope. As soon as he calmed Joel down and explained what he required of the man, Nick could spend the rest of the night tailing an unsuspecting Cory.

The minute he entered Joel's plush office at the lodge headquarters, the man bolted from his seat behind the massive wooden desk. "What have you done with her?" he roared. "And don't give me any more of that bullshit about Lake Tahoe. I have friends in Tahoe, and if she was there, I'd have found her by now."

Nick was tired and he was disgusted. "Shut up and sit down and I'll tell you," he snarled.

Joel did, but his jaw jutted out at a dangerous angle. "Make it good," he said.

"She's been kidnapped. That good enough for you?"

"If you won't tell me the truth, I'll just have to…" Joel's eyes widened. "You're serious."

Nick nodded. "Two nights ago. They left a note that basically said 'no police.' I've been waiting for instructions."

"Who would do such a thing?"

"I don't know. When I do…" Nick smacked a fist against an open palm, thinking grim thoughts about Cory.

Joel leaned forward. "What can I do to help? Anything! Name it."

"Keep quiet, stay out of my way and don't be surprised if I suddenly disappear. That'll mean I'm on to something."

The man looked torn. "Are you sure it wouldn't be better to contact the police? They have resources—"

"You haven't been listening. The note said no cops. We have no idea what we're dealing with here. Do you want to take that chance?"

The air seemed to rush out of the man and his shoulders slumped. "Of course not. I'd never do anything to endanger Sammy."

"Yeah," Nick said. "Sammy." He rose. "I can count on you, then?"

"You can count on me."

"Good, because there's one other thing—"

"Name it."

"If you're contacted by anyone from the Spade Insurance Agency, do exactly what they tell you to do, no questions asked."

The man's eyes grew wide. "Like what?"

"Like hold on to anything they may send you, provide anything they may request." Nick headed for the door. "They'll only contact you if I'm not around, so don't worry too much about it. Just remember that this is serious business, and keep your mouth shut. Think you can do that?"

"For Sammy? Yeah, I can do that."

Satisfied, Nick walked back to Cory's bungalow in gathering darkness, intensely aware that time was running out. Since she was due to leave tomorrow, something should happen tonight, if his hunch was right. There'd been only an hour's lapse in surveillance, but if she thought he was out of the picture until morning…

He stopped short. There wasn't a light anywhere in her bungalow. Had she run out on him already? Son of a—!

Swearing under his breath, he whipped around and headed for his own bungalow, figuring there was at least a long shot that any *business* she had would be there.

CORY STOOD AT NICK'S bungalow door, wallowing in disappointment. How could he go off without her that way? Tomorrow loomed like a mushroom cloud over the placid landscape of her vacation. She'd tried to push reality out of her mind in favor of romantic fantasy but now she was going to have to face facts.

Though not until tomorrow, if she could help it.

The door was locked, but she'd expected that and had a contingency plan. Slipping into the shadows at one side of the small structure, she moved through moonlight and shadows from one window to the next, quickly locating one that was unlocked. It took her no time at all to remove the screen and climb inside.

She found herself in a bedroom. She had a plan for this, too. She'd just take off her clothes and crawl into bed to wait for Nick to—

The door slammed open and lights flashed on almost simultaneously. Nick stood in the doorway, but not a Nick she knew.

He was practically breathing fire. "What the hell are you doing here?" he yelled at her. "What are you looking for?"

"I'm looking for you—what do you think?" She took a hasty step back. That angry gleam in his eyes alarmed her.

"Yeah, and I'm selling swampland in Florida." He advanced on her.

"Oh, Nick!" She frowned. "I know I shouldn't have broken in, but I wanted to surprise you. I'm leaving tomorrow—"

"So you had to do your dirty work tonight, is that it?"

"W-what dirty work?"

"Hell, Cory," he snarled, without the slightest warmth in his voice, "why don't you just tell me where Samantha is and maybe we can call ourselves even."

"Isn't she in Tahoe? That's what you said."

"But you knew it was a lie." He advanced on her. "Who's behind this? It'll go easier with you if you tell me now."

"Behind what?" Her heart banged anxiously against her ribs. He was talking crazy, but he was acting dead serious.

"Okay, we'll play it your way." His lip curled. "Take your clothes off."

She gasped. "Take my…? Are you joking?" She tried to back away from him.

"Take 'em off."

"Why should I?"

"Isn't that what you claim you're here for? To seduce me?"

"Yes, but—"

"So take your clothes off. Look, I'm going to search you whether you like it or not."

"I *don't* like it! When I take my clothes off, it'll be because I want to, not because some arrogant jerk tells me to." But of course, that was exactly why she was here: to take her clothes off.

"Spare me the maidenly modesty, Cory."

He reached for her. She ducked, but not fast enough. He grabbed her arm just above the elbow and foiled her escape. She turned on him with a flurry of blows that he barely seemed to notice. He sat down on the bed and pulled her into his lap.

Despite her best efforts to resist, he soon had her pinned to his chest with one arm. "You're just making this hard on yourself," he panted.

"I'm making this hard on *you*." She lunged, but couldn't escape his harsh grip. "My God, Nick, why are you doing this to me?"

"Because I don't like having people snatched out from under my nose."

With his free hand, he grabbed the front of her semisheer, white cotton blouse. He yanked and the delicate fabric gave without protest, buttons flying everywhere.

She shrieked and renewed her efforts to escape. "Do you have any idea what this blouse cost?" she yelled at him. "Stop it, you brute!"

He fought to control her. "Hold still, damn it! I don't want to hurt you, but—" He stopped speaking abruptly.

She stopped struggling just as abruptly. "But you will if you have to—is that what you were about to say?"

"Something like that." It was a surly, mumbled response.

She supposed that was something—not much, but something. "If I don't cooperate, you're going to rip everything I'm wearing to shreds, is that it?"

"Yeah. That's about it." His blue eyes hardened again.

"In that case, turn me loose."

"Forget it."

"No, really. Turn me loose. I won't run."

He did, reluctantly. She stood up very slowly, then turned to face him where he still sat on the side of the bed. She held her arms out to the side, her beautiful breasts on display between the ragged edges of the blouse.

"All right," she said coldly. "Search me."

He licked his lips, and for a moment she thought he would relent. Instead he slipped the blouse from her shoulders, dragging it down her arms. Crumpling it between his hands, he examined every inch by feel. Then he looked it over with equal care before tossing it aside.

And all that time, Cory stood there in front of him, practically naked to the waist with her breasts just at mouth level. She felt her nipples grow tight and hard and she drew in a shallow breath, telling herself to rise above this indignity. He wasn't interested in her body, probably never had been. He'd been using her, nothing more.

She found herself staring at a corner of the ceiling, where two walls met. *Stand still and think of England,* she harangued herself silently. This would soon be over and she'd never have to see this brute again.

Never feel his hands on her again—

His hands on her waist snapped her back to the present. "What are you doing?" she cried in alarm.

"Searching you."

He didn't look up. She stared down at the top of his dark head while he worked on the snap and zipper of her white linen pants. Now that she hated him, she expected to be repelled by his touch.

She wasn't. If anything, the situation added an extra element of...dangerous suspense. He tugged impatiently. With a ripping sound, the pants slid down over her hips. She stood before him in bra, panties and sandals, shivering but not cold. He glanced up at her once, his eyes opaque and his mouth a hard thin line. Then he slid a hand behind one of her knees and lifted.

She caught her breath, but he was only pulling the pant leg free. Again he examined every inch of fabric, then tossed the linen pants aside.

"Turn around," he said.

Rebellion surged through her, but what was the point? Stiffly she did as he'd ordered. His hands between her shoulder blades shocked her, and then the bra fell free. His hands slipped beneath the elastic of her panties to peel them down. Mouth dry with humiliation—or maybe with arousal—she kept her shoulders rigid and her chin up.

This would soon be over. He would find nothing incriminating because there was nothing to find. He'd realize he was wrong about her, but she would never forgive him for...

His arms slipped around her and he cupped her breasts with his hands, cutting off all rational thought on her part. "What are you doing?" she gasped. "That's not fair, Nick," She covered his hands with hers and tried to pry them away, succeeding only in pressing them closer.

"I had to do it." He sounded agonized by the admission. "I had to search you."

Sitting down again, he pulled her with him. Before she knew what was happening, she found herself straddling his thighs with her back still toward him. Pressing kisses between her shoulder blades, he continued to knead her breasts until she melted into a quivering mass of indecision.

"If you think I'm going to make love with a man who's just humiliated me, you've got the wrong woman," she panted, trying to bend away from him.

"But this is what you came for, or so you said." Clamping an arm beneath her breasts, he slid a hand down over her belly to the point where her thighs separated.

"That was before..." She lost her train of thought and gasped. He'd found the spot that rendered her helpless to resist. "Don't...please, don't!"

"Don't what?" A second finger joined the first.

"Don't...stop!"

And he didn't, not for a long, long time....

SHE LAY PROPPED against the pillows, staring straight into his eyes. "You misjudged me. You owe me an apology."

It came out low and sexy, yanking Nick out of his glow of satisfaction. "That has yet to be established."

Her eyes widened. "You're kidding!"

"Okay, I'm kidding." Uncomfortable because of what had just transpired between them, he swung his legs over the side of the bed and sat up. He shouldn't have taken her that way, but he'd felt so rotten for accusing her, and so glad he hadn't found anything incriminating, that for a moment he'd pushed aside the name *Laura* and...

His gaze settled on a small black shoulder bag lying half under the bed, where they'd apparently kicked it. "Is that your purse?" he asked suddenly.

"Is what my purse?"

"Down there." He pointed. "It's black, opens on top, has a long strap."

"Good grief, I wondered where that had gone." She scooted over so she could see.

Leaning down, he snagged the strap and hauled the bag within reach. She grabbed for it, but he held it away from her.

"You didn't bring it with you just now?"

"Of course not. That's an evening… What are you *doing?*"

"What does it look like?" He dumped the contents of the bag on the bed between them and began pawing through them.

"But you can't just go through my purse. That's my property."

"Have you got something to hide?" He tossed aside a lipstick and mirror.

"Of course not, but that's my personal, private purse. You can't just—"

She made a grab, but he batted her hands aside. Tissues, nail file, comb—checking off each item, he tossed them back into the purse while she glared at him.

A business card from a Houston restaurant, a tiny gold pen, a scrap of newspaper—

"What's this?" He smoothed the bit of newsprint on the bed before him.

"Let me see." She craned her neck to get a better look, then sat back. "That's not mine."

"It was in your purse."

"Then somebody put it there."

He gave her a quelling glance. The bittersweet euphoria of their wild joining had worn off while his doubts mushroomed. "This looks like something about Nevada ghost towns. Pioche, Hiko, Rhyolite—"

She shook her head stubbornly. "That's not mine. I don't know anything about Nevada ghost towns and care less."

"Goldfield, Silverpeak—"

"I'll bet you read cereal boxes."

"—Black Bird!"

She stiffened. "Black Bird?"

He smoothed the paper and read. "'Once a thriving mining center, now a remote ghost town in the middle of nowhere. So difficult to reach that few people go there. No clear consensus on the best route. Better to avoid this one.'"

"Oh, darn," she said, "and my heart was set on—"

"That's where they're holding Samantha."

"Samantha? But why would anybody…" She gasped. "Do you suppose this has anything to do with Laura?"

Nick caught Cory's wrist in a hard grip and dragged her close. "Don't tell me you pulled that name out of a hat."

"I…why I…"

He saw in her eyes the knowledge that she was in big trouble.

8

"OKAY, THAT DOES IT!" Nick got right in Cory's face, so angry that it was all he could do to keep his hands off her. "I'm going to Black Bird and you're coming with me."

"Don't be ridiculous." She tried to shove him away.

"That's what you think." Standing up, he dragged her off the bed and stood her on her feet. "Get dressed."

"In what?" She glared at him, clutching the sheet across her breasts. "You ripped my clothes to shreds, remember?"

"Damn!" He glanced around the room and realized it was Samantha's. Inspiration struck. "There's a closet full of stuff. Take whatever you need."

Instead, Cory bent to pick up her slacks, but he stopped her by stepping on the puddle of fabric. "Wait a minute. If you wear Samantha's stuff, nobody will even know Cory Leblanc is with me."

"Wait just a minute here." She backed away, her eyes growing wide. "Why would you care if anybody knows I'm with you unless..." Whirling, she bolted for the door.

He caught one flying corner of the sheet and

reeled her in. "Calm down. I'm not going to hurt you."

"Oh, sure," she sneered. "You're about to kidnap me and I'm supposed to believe you have my best interests at heart? I don't think so!"

"I don't care what you think," he said in the most dangerous tone he could summon. "Get dressed or I'll carry you out of here buck naked. How'd you like that?"

"Not much," she admitted. "What if I swear that I know nothing about Samantha's disappearance, that I'm an innocent bystander?"

"You know about Laura."

"Well, yeah." Cory's guilty expression would have been amusing under other circumstances. "What happened was I overheard you and Samantha talking in here one night. I didn't say anything because I was ashamed to be eavesdropping."

He remembered; it was the night he'd lost his money clip at her front door. "You heard a lot more than that," he accused.

"Not a *lot*." She licked lips bare of artificial color. "Just that Samantha owns an insurance agency and you're one of her agents. I didn't stay very long, honest."

"You expect me to believe that?" Laura! She *was* Laura. "Get dressed. You can come peacefully or you can come not so peacefully, but you *will* come."

It looked as if she would argue. Instead she gritted her teeth and turned toward the closet, but he'd seen her expression.

The fight wasn't over.

CORY DELIBERATELY CHOSE an outfit that no one except Samantha would—or could—wear without looking like some kind of nut: white crepe, wide-legged pants and a matching midriff-baring shirt. A flowering vine stenciled in muted, misty colors trailed from the right shoulder across the shirt and down the left pant leg.

"Hurry it up, will you?"

Busy buckling a pair of Samantha's high-heeled sandals around her ankles, Cory didn't even glance up at the Beast of La Paloma. If Nick wanted her to dress like Samantha, she'd *dress* like Samantha. Whipping a white chiffon scarf from a closet hook, she twined it around her head and neck, clapped on a pair of oversize sunglasses and faced him defiantly.

His jaw dropped. "Jeez, red lipstick and you could pass for *her*."

Cory snapped her fingers. "Red lipstick—right. In the bathroom?"

She emerged seconds later, the transformation complete. Actually, although she glared at him, she was secretly delighted. Maybe in Samantha's case, clothes really did make the woman. They sure made Cory look, as well as feel, different!

The way Nick kept staring at her was beginning to make her uneasy, though. "Look," she said in a placating tone, "this is really ridiculous. If Samantha's been kidnapped, why haven't we seen police around here investigating?"

"The kidnappers' note said no police or—" He drew a forefinger across his throat with appropriate sound effects.

"That's silly. Let's go to the police now."

"We're going to Black Bird."

"We don't even know where Black Bird is."

"It's in Nevada. We'll find it." He hustled her toward the door. "I've just got to grab a few things."

Her antennae shot up. "Things?"

They entered the other bedroom. Keeping one eye on her and the other on what he was doing, he hauled a small flight bag off a shelf. Opening a false bottom, he extracted a pistol from a secret compartment.

"Things," Cory said weakly. She'd never been this close to a real gun before.

He shoved the barrel into the waistband of his trousers, settling the tails of his aloha shirt to cover it. "You ready?"

"Nick, don't do this! It's kidnapping. Besides, when I'm not on that airplane—"

"Nobody will even notice." He advanced on her. "Parents dead, fiancé dumped, no boss expecting you back at work."

Even Crystal probably wouldn't notice; she'd probably think Cory had run away with the handsome stranger. "When you put it that way, I might as *well* go with you," she said with ill grace.

Was that a slight relaxation of his stiff shoulders?

"Yeah, well, just be a good girl and nobody'll get hurt."

In all honesty, it had never occurred to her that he'd actually hurt her. She might, however, have to put him to the test.

THE ONLY ROUTE to the parking lot where the rented convertible waited was through the lobby.

Nick didn't think she'd try anything, but he wasn't taking any chances if he could help it.

Still reeling from shock at her resemblance to Samantha, he clutched her elbow in a heavy grip and steered her into the lobby, past the desk and the waterfall. She walked stiffly, keeping her attention focused straight ahead. They were nearing the large glass doors, almost home free—

"Sammy?"

At Joel's delighted cry, Nick started, his grip on her arm loosening. At that very instant, Cory bounded forward, her first scream lost in the jingle of coins in slot machines and the rush of water.

He was upon her before she reached the door. Grabbing her, he swung her around in a circle and got a glimpse of wide-eyed alarm, of a mouth wide-open to scream again.

Naturally, he did the only thing he knew to be as effective as a slap in such circumstances: he kissed her. Bending her before him, he kissed her with all the rage and frustration that had been building since he'd let his boss get snatched from beneath his nose.

The blows raining on his shoulders ceased abruptly. Wrapping her arms around his neck, Cory opened her mouth and invited him in.

A hand on his arm dragged Nick around. Joel Caspar stood there, his face an angry red.

"You son of a bitch," he growled. "You told me Sammy was..." He glanced at Cory and did a double take. "Jesus, is that you, Sammy? What the hell's going on here?"

Cory whipped off her dark glasses. "It's me, Mr. Caspar," she hissed. "I'm being kidnapped! Call the police! Call the FBI!"

Joel looked completely flummoxed. "But the way you're dressed—I don't get this."

Nick shoved an arm around the waist of the totally unfathomable woman. "This is Cory Leblanc. She's in on it."

"You mean, in on Sammy's kidnapping?" Joel looked stunned. "Is she on our side or *their* side?"

"My guess is theirs. Look, I've got a lead." Nick thrust the scrap of newspaper into Joel's hands. "I want you to put this in the safe until I get back."

"What is it?"

"Never mind that, just keep it safe, along with anything else that comes for me."

"The police—"

"No police!"

Joel swallowed hard, then nodded. "And Ms. Leblanc?"

"She's coming with me. If I don't find Samantha alive and well, somebody's got to pay." He dug his fingers into Cory's side. She gasped and gave him an indignant look.

"He's lying! I'm an innocent bystander. He made me put on these clothes after he—"

Nick saw her hesitate over explaining how her own clothes had been ripped from her body, after which she'd made love to the ripper. "Look, Caspar," he said, "if anyone asks, I left here tonight with Samantha. Last I heard of Corinne Leblanc, she was on her way to Las Vegas to meet her uncle Mario. You got that?"

Joel's moral battle was evident in his expression. Then he nodded. "I got it. Keep me posted, all right?"

"If I can." Nick turned away. "You ever been to a place called Black Bird?"

"Never even heard of it. Is it in Nevada?"

For all Nick knew, it could be in hell.

CORY SLUMPED in the red convertible, her head tilted back against the seat. Above her, a million stars glittered in a black velvet sky. Wind rushed through her hair and tugged at the chiffon scarf she held on her lap. She fancied that the faint scent on the soft night air was sage.

She fancied that the man beside her, driving with total concentration and completely ignoring her, hadn't just shocked her silly.

The kiss in the lobby had been a real barn burner, full of the usual desire but spiced with a fury that had riveted her to the spot. When Joel broke it up, she'd tried to get back her outrage at being summarily kidnapped, but had been unable to do so. When Nick hustled her out of the lobby and through the parking lot, she'd submitted almost meekly.

Why? She was no quitter. She—

"Are you awake?"

She started at the sound of his voice. "Do you think I can sleep when I'm being kidnapped?"

He made no reply. She glared at him for a few moments, then looked back up at the sky as if she could find answers there.

Her first question was why? Why had she come along with him on this wild-goose chase when she could have screamed down the place, back in the resort lobby?

Because, she decided, she was crazed. Either that or... She let out her breath in consternation. Either crazed or in love. But how could she have fallen in love in these few days? There had to be a better answer.

Maybe her yen for adventure had kicked in. She'd come looking for, dreaming of, romance and adventure. Nick had given her romance, and now he was offering her adventure—actually thrusting it upon her.

She'd be a fool to pass up such a chance.

She rolled her head to the side so she could see him in the green glow of the dash lights. "Do you know where we're going?"

"Black Bird."

"Yes, but do you know where that is?"

"North. That's all I got out of that crummy little clipping."

"Didn't the newspaper say it was hard to find? Wandering around in the dark doesn't seem too smart to me."

"Will you shut up and go to sleep or something?"

"I will not. It was *your* idea to drag me along. The least you can do is tell me how you expect to keep from getting us hopelessly lost."

"We're going to stop for the night, okay?" He kept his eyes straight ahead. "Tomorrow we'll find one of those maps that show ghost towns. It'll be simple. Now shut up and let me drive."

She shut up, but she was thinking, *You and me alone in a motel room? It won't be simple!*

HE REGISTERED THEM at a seedy motel as Mr. and
Mrs. Nicholas Charles, after warning her of the
direst consequences if she caused a scene. Standing meekly at his side, she stifled a smile.

The skinny night-desk clerk hadn't taken his
eyes off her since she entered. She supposed she
was quite a sight in her borrowed finery, dark
glasses perched on her nose at midnight.

She smiled at the clerk and said in her best Samantha tone, part sarcasm, part superiority,
"Nice place you got here."

The clerk gulped and nodded. "Yeah. You folks
coming in from Vegas?"

"That's ri—"

"Carson City." Nick cut her off with a warning
glance. "We're on our way to Las Vegas." He
pushed the register across the counter.

The clerk dangled the key from his fingers.
"Hope you enjoy your stay with us…" he glanced
at Nick's scrawl "…Mr. and Mrs. Charles. You're
in number nine. We'll have coffee here tomorrow
morning if you want to drop by. Any problems,
just holler."

Cory smiled sweetly. "Holler, you say?"

Nick squeezed her arm. "We'll do that. Com'
on, honey. It's been a real long day."

And it's not even over, Cory thought, following
him out the door.

NUMBER NINE WAS A symphony in squalor. The
bedspread was so worn that it was no longer possible to discern a color, two out of three knobs
were missing from the television set and the two

folded towels stacked on the rickety dresser were approximately one inch thick, total.

Cory entered first, looking around with exaggerated disdain. "All the comforts of home," she announced.

"Nag, nag, nag." Nick dropped the key on the bedside table and plopped down on the side of the bed.

"Don't do that!"

He started. "Do what?"

"Sit on a motel bedspread, especially a motel like this one." Rushing to the opposite side of the bed, she tugged at the spread.

After a stubborn moment, he stood up long enough for her to drag the offending item from the bed entirely.

"Why the hell did you do that?" he demanded in a plaintive voice.

She rubbed her hands together as if cleaning them. "I read an article that said motel bedspreads were tested for cleanliness and the things they found were disgusting."

He looked interested. "Like what?"

"You don't want to know!"

"Yes, I do."

"Think about it, then. What do you suppose most people use motel beds for?"

He considered. "I'd guess 'sleeping' isn't the correct answer," he ventured.

"Ha!" She sat gingerly in the only chair in the room, even if it did look like a Salvation Army reject.

He stood to unbutton his aloha shirt, the pistol butt protruding from his waistband. "Sorry this place doesn't meet your high standards, but desperate times call for desperate measures.''

"What have you got to be desperate about? Great big man with a great big gun..." She sniffed haughtily. "You're a bully, you know that? And a liar and a kidnapper—''

He yawned and sat back down on the edge of the bed. "Stop before you hurt my feelings." He tossed the shirt in the general direction of the dresser. "I'm bushed and I'm going to bed. You coming or do you want to sit in that chair all night?''

She considered. Lie on that bed with a man she loved making love with but now wouldn't touch with a ten-foot pole, or sit up all night on this grimy, spring-busted chair? "Why don't I take the bed and you take the chair?" she ventured.

"In your dreams." He stretched out on the bed, crossing long legs in khaki trousers, bending his arms to cradle his head on a pillow so flat it might as well have been an empty case.

She chewed on her lower lip. "I guess I don't have much choice," she grumbled. "But before I get close to that bed, we've got to get a few things straight.''

"Such as?''

"I want it clearly understood that I am here under duress.''

"Okay. Get in the bed.''

"Not quite yet! I also want it clearly understood that there's to be no hanky-panky.''

"Hanky-panky?" For a moment he stared at her, then burst out laughing. "You mean sex?''

She gritted her teeth. "That's exactly what I

mean. We're finished. You used me. I've never been so humiliated—''

"Get over it, Cory." His steely voice cut through her lamentations. "If there was any 'using' done, it was the other way around. Why don't you come clean?"

She lifted her chin defensively. "I don't know what you mean."

"The hell you don't." He swung his legs across the bed and sat up, her chair so close that their knees touched. "How did you get mixed up in this? If you tell me all you know, it'll go easier for you in the long run."

For a minute they stared into each other's eyes. Then she pulled back sharply. "I got mixed up in this because the minute I saw you in the lobby that first day, I thought you were the sexiest man alive. I swear it on a stack of Bibles."

He looked taken aback. "You're kidding."

"Nick..." She shook her head helplessly. He'd made up his mind and she'd never be able to change it.

He yanked open the small drawer in the rickety table and pulled out the Gideon Bible, thrusting it toward her. "Swear."

Without the slightest hesitation, she put her right hand on the book and raised her left, then reversed hands, frowned, shrugged, put both hands on the Bible and spoke in measured tones. "I, Corinne Leblanc of Houston, Texas, do hereby swear that I know nothing about the alleged disappearance of Samantha Spade, had nothing to do with it, and if I *did* know anything about it I'd spill my guts."

For another minute they sat there, him holding the Bible and her in "swearing" position.

Then she let out her breath in a long sigh. "You believe me, right?"

He replaced the Bible in the drawer and closed it. "Either you're telling the truth or—"

"Or what?" she cried in frustration.

"Or you're even better than I thought you were...and I thought you were very, very good."

"You *don't* believe me."

"Let's just say I need time to think about it."

She glared in disappointment. "And on that sorry note, we've got to crawl into bed together."

"Hell, it's not the first time. What's your problem?"

"As if you didn't know." She clenched her fists. "If you touch me, Nicholas Charles, I'll scream so loud they'll hear me all the way to Las Vegas."

"I have no intention of touching you—any more than I have to, anyway."

She recoiled. "Have to?"

"Can't let you skip out on me before I find Samantha. You could be the only bargaining chip I have."

Cory stared at him in disbelief. What kind of woman did he think she was? And then she realized that he thought she was the kind of woman who'd sleep with a man to distract him from the criminal activities of her confederates.

"Fine," she snapped, "that's just fine." She held out crisscrossed wrists. "What do you plan to do, tie me to the bedposts?"

"Nope," he said, "although that idea has considerable appeal. I'm planning to tie you to *me*."

FOR A LONG TIME, Cory lay there seething in the dark, her right ankle bound to Nick's left ankle by a thin strip of fabric torn from the ragged edge of the top sheet. If Crystal could see her now!

If Crystal could see her now…in a cheap motel in the middle of Nevada, physically bound to a handsome man who'd been her lover but was now her captor…

Cory shivered with suppressed pleasure. If Crystal could see her now, she'd envy the adventure into which Cory had been plunged. Little Corinne Leblanc, to whom nothing exciting had *ever* happened, was embarked upon the adventure of a lifetime.

Be careful what you wish for, her mother had often warned when Cory complained about the narrow parameters of her life. *You may get it.* Cory had wished fervently for two things. She'd already had the first: romance. And if this wasn't the second—adventure—she didn't know what was.

Why on earth would she want to go back to Houston before this scenario was played out? She, too, wanted to know what had happened to Wil Archer and Samantha Spade, assuming anything actually had. Then, more than anything, she wanted to rub Nick's nose in her innocence.

Drowsy at last, she sighed and cupped one hand beneath her cheek. Tomorrow she'd offer him a deal: she'd promise not to try to "escape" if he'd stop tying her up and start treating her like a partner in this enterprise. Yes, that's what she'd do…and together they'd solve the mystery of the disappearing…

She slept.

Nick didn't, although he was exhausted and pretended he did.

He heard her breathing grow relaxed beside him, punctuated now and then by a sigh. What was she dreaming? That she and her henchmen…

Hell, she didn't have any henchmen. In spite of how it looked, in spite of her fumbling attempts to explain why she knew things she shouldn't, he didn't really believe she was one of the bad guys. Of course, there was always that outside chance….

He shifted slightly, trying not to tug at the soft binding between his ankle and hers. She slid against him as if he'd planned it that way, her smooth cheek coming to rest against the curve of his shoulder.

Could she be the missing Laura and not even know it? But if she didn't know it, why was she here, since Uncle Mario was obviously just a cover story?

She *had* to know.

Or maybe she was an innocent victim for the second time….

At which point, a horrible possibility occurred to him: he'd completely lost his objectivity. He didn't *want* her to be mixed up in all this, and as a result, he wasn't thinking straight. What he wanted was to send her back to Las Vegas with orders to get the hell out of Nevada and never come back. Maybe then she'd be safe….

Or so he told himself as he finally drifted off to sleep.

When he awakened, she was gone.

9

NICK ROLLED OUT OF BED swearing horribly, the cotton thong dangling from his left ankle. How had she managed to get loose? Now he'd have to find her, and she'd already cost him enough time—

The front door banged open and she stood there, a darker form framed by the grayness of early morning light. Before he could react, she walked inside, closing the door with a smart backward kick.

"Good morning." She held out a small tray for his perusal. "I brought us some—" She stopped speaking abruptly. "My God, what is it? You look like…" Understanding dawned. "You thought I was gone!" This seemed to amuse her greatly.

He rubbed sandy eyes and spoke in a sandy voice. "It occurred to me."

"Thanks, thanks a lot!" She set the tray down on the bedside table so hard that coffee sloshed over the rims of the cups. "Here I am, trying to be nice—"

"Can it." He reached for a coffee. "You made it clear last night that the first chance you got, you were gone. Can you blame me for thinking I'd seen the last of you?"

She grimaced. "I suppose not." Picking up the

other cup, she gave him an oblique glance. "Would you have come after me?"

"What do you think?"

Her sunny smile said she thought he would. "Anyway," she said, "I've changed my mind. I'm staying to clear my name."

"What if I've changed *my* mind and decided to let you go?"

"I don't want to go."

"Last night you said—"

"I know, but I've decided I want to see this thing through to the end. To clear my name, like I said."

He stared at her through narrowed eyes. This didn't make any sense that he could see. He *had* kidnapped her. Why did she want to stick around all of a sudden—unless it was part of some nefarious scheme?

"Care for a doughnut?" she asked.

Okay, change the subject. "Sure."

"They're hard as rocks, but we can always dunk 'em." She picked up a paper plate and held it toward him, offering him first choice of the five hard, skinny doughnuts piled there. He reached for the chocolate, but his glance snagged on an envelope on the tray, previously concealed by the plate. He picked up the doughnut with one hand and the envelope with his name scrawled on it with the other.

"What's this?" he asked.

"The desk clerk sent it to you."

Nick's blood ran cold. "A telephone message? No one knows we're here unless..."

She looked startled. "I thought it was just a receipt or something."

"But you don't know." How dumb did she think he was? In her shoes, he'd have opened it in a New York minute.

"How would I know? He sent it to you, not me."

Nick took a bite of doughnut, which wasn't easy considering how hard that sucker was. He waved the envelope gently in her direction. "You weren't even tempted to cop a peek?"

"No." Her eyes went wide. "Do you really think that's a note about Samantha's disappearance? *Nick, open it!*"

He opened it and read aloud: "You're only half as dumb as you look, gumshoe. Black Bird. Bring the babe. Cultivate patience."

CORY STOOD IN A NARROW aisle of the Falcon Mercantile and Dry Goods Emporium, her lip thrust out in protest. "But I don't want a pair of cowboy boots," she insisted. "And I don't want one of those silly hats. Jeans and shirt, okay, but the rest—"

"Wrap it up with the other stuff," Nick instructed the clerk, "and throw in a handful of bandannas, two canteens, a couple of Swiss Army knives, toothbrushes—"

"Where do you think we're going," Cory griped, "the Outback? Nevada may not have a lot of people, but it *is* a civilized state."

"—two flashlights, a box of those energy bars, some chocolate, a couple of blankets."

The clerk, a short, lean individual with gray

hair cut so short it looked more like bristles, gave Cory an amused glance. "Little lady's got a point," he said, moving behind the counter to begin ringing up the items. "Where *are* you folks headed?"

"Ever hear of a town called Black Bird?"

"Sure, but why would you want to go there?"

"To take the waters," Cory suggested wryly.

"Were we misinformed?" Nick shot her a baleful glance.

"Actually," the clerk said, hitting the Total key, "you weren't. Folks who've been there say it's got kind of a...you know, one'a them desert spots with water?"

"Oasis?" Cory guessed.

"That's it, an oasis just outside of town."

"You ever been there?" Nick pulled out his wallet.

"Me? Not since I was a pup."

"Long way from Falcon, I guess." Nick counted out bills.

"Not really. Maybe a hundred miles northeast. But folks who been there lately—that's in the last twenty years or so—say the trip's a bitch. Road washed out years ago and you have to follow trails. Then when you make it, you're about as welcome as fleas on a dog."

"People live there?" Cory asked in surprise. "I thought it was a ghost town."

The clerk shrugged. "Ghosts live there, too, little lady, and there's always prospectors wandering around lookin' to strike it rich. I also heard a while back that there's a couple'a strange types took up residence in the old Black Bird Hotel.

Claim to be some kinda scientists or writers or something. From what I hear, they're crazy as bedbugs and about as friendly."

Nick handed Cory the smaller of the two packages. "Was Black Bird much in its day?"

The clerk scratched his chin. "It was no Virginia City or Rhyolite, but it had a few good years—twenty, maybe. Silver started it, but they run into a vein of gold real fast. Had the usual get-rich-quickers pouring in from all over the country. The town boomed overnight and died just as fast when the gold petered out."

Nick hoisted the larger package off the counter. "If we decide to stop by Black Bird, how's the best way to get there?"

The clerk pursed his lips thoughtfully. "I reckon by way of Cairo would be the your best bet," he said at last. "It's only about ten miles from Black Bird, but that's ten hard miles. You got a' off-road vehicle? You might make it that way. Otherwise…" He shook his head decisively.

"It was just an idea." Nick turned toward the door. "Maybe we'll just go on to Virginia City."

"Prob'ly best."

"But—"

"Com' on, Cory."

"But—"

"Come *on*, Cory." Nick hustled her out of the store.

THE MAN WAS MADE for cowboy clothes.

Standing beside the unmade motel bed, Cory stared at Nick with fresh admiration. She'd never in her life seen anybody who looked better in a pair of jeans. And whereas she felt downright silly in the high-heeled boots, he looked and moved as if he'd been wearing them all his life.

Which she knew he hadn't. He was a city boy from San Francisco, for heaven's sake, maybe a drugstore cowboy. Now that she thought about it, even his voice seemed different now...slower, with a kind of easy drawl.

"Nick," she said impulsively, "who *are* you...really?"

His hands stilled on the strip of leather he'd been buckling around his lean hips. "I'm a professional bodyguard from San Francisco by way of Oklahoma. Who the hell are *you?*"

She sat down hard on the side of the unmade bed. She wanted to laugh, to tell him his joke was funny, but somehow she knew the instant she heard the words that they were true.

"Well?" he demanded. "Aren't you going to answer my question?"

She drew in a distressed breath. "I'm exactly who I said I was and exactly what I seem to be."

"Ah, there's the rub." He sat in the chair in front of her. "One minute you *seem* to be one thing and the next minute another. At first I thought you were just a hot babe. Then I decided you were a sweet kid from an overprotective family. Then I suspected you were a decoy sent to take my mind off business. Now I have to wonder..." He regarded her with brooding eyes. "I guess you get the idea."

It was a revelation to her that anyone could think her capable of such...cunning! Also flattering, in a way.... "You saw all those possibilities in me? Simple little me?"

"Yeah, and I'm not sure that's past tense," he growled. "Cory, if you're holding anything back, now's the time to come clean."

She shook her head vehemently. "I'm not and that's the truth."

He sighed. "Time will tell, I guess."

"It always does." She chewed on her lip, remembering all she'd overheard that fateful night outside his window. "Are you *really* a bodyguard? I thought you worked for Samantha's insurance agency."

He smiled, and it transformed his face. "I do, but the agency is a front to guard the privacy of her personal-protection clientele. That's why I knew Jennifer Jordan. I spent a couple of months guarding her from a stalker last year."

"She was very...grateful."

"Most people are grateful when they think you've saved their life."

"Did you? Save her life, I mean."

He shrugged. "It's possible."

"And Samantha. Were you guarding her when she disappeared?"

He rose and walked to the tiny window with its gray curtain. "Not really. She brought me along to keep her from committing murder when she found out—" He stopped and rounded on the woman sitting on the bed. "You overheard us talking about Samantha's daughter. Both Samantha and Wil got notes that mentioned Laura."

"Was that a ruse to get them here, do you think? I mean, why would the people who took

Laura want to kidnap Samantha and Wil after all these years?"

"God only knows. But they would give everything they own to find out if Laura is still alive, and why she was taken."

Cory felt tears clog the back of her throat. "And you think I'd be part of a scheme to torture these people? Nick, how could you?"

He seemed to waver in his resolve. For a moment she thought he'd lift her from the bed and into his arms—in which case, of course, she'd be forced to slap his face before she kissed him. Instead, he thrust his hands deep into the pockets of his jeans and rocked back on his boot heels.

"I don't know what to think about you at the moment," he said, his expression grim. "Not that it matters. The bad guys know you're with me. I've got no choice now but to take you along."

She clenched her teeth so tightly that her jaw ached. "Just try to get rid of me," she said angrily. "I have a few things to prove myself."

"Then I have your word you won't try to escape?"

She glared at him. "I *want* to stay. Do I have your word that when you finally realize you've misjudged me, you'll get down on your hands and knees and apologize?"

"Sure." He tossed it out carelessly. "Assuming I'm able."

"You don't really expect me to believe that we're in any danger!"

He grabbed her elbows and yanked her off the bed, glaring into her startled eyes. "Listen and listen good. This is no joke and it's not your dream of adventure. We're dealing with dangerous people here—probably the same people who stole a helpless baby from her mother's arms. Somebody may get hurt—hell, somebody may already be hurt, or even dead.''

"You don't think Samantha or Wil—"

"I don't know *what* to think. This is the most cockamamie case I ever worked on. If I had a choice, I sure as hell wouldn't want some ditzy female I can't even trust tagging along. I'm warning you—"

He stopped short. "I keep forgetting that you probably know more about this than I do. So yeah, if I'm wrong about you I'll apologize—"

"On your hands and knees!"

"—on my hands and knees. But if I'm right about you, I hope there's someone around to keep me from putting my hands around your pretty neck."

Deliberately he slid his hands up her arms and across her shoulders to curve around her vulnerable throat. His expression said he was serious; her reaction said he wasn't.

"You don't scare me, Nick Charles." She flung off his hands. "And just for the record…"

"Yeah?"

"I realize you probably sleep with all your suspects, but it'll be a cold day before you get *me* between the sheets again. From here on out, it's strictly business."

As they loaded their meager possessions into the rental car, she looked up into the trackless sky that heralded another blazingly hot day and wondered how much of what she'd said was really true.

THEY DROVE INTO CAIRO, Nevada, at one that afternoon, after miles and miles of nothing but sand and sagebrush. There'd been no conversation and no radio, because no stations were within reach.

Cairo was no particular improvement over Falcon. A rundown little town with weeds growing through cracked sidewalks, and a motley collection of weather-beaten homes, it was little more than a wide spot in the road.

Nick pulled into the first service station he saw, an ancient affair with old-fashioned round gasoline pumps. An assortment of broken-down vehicles clogged the entrance to the service bay. While he pumped gas, Cory opened her car door in hopes that any kind of breeze would find her.

The attendant, a young man in greasy coveralls, ambled out of the service bay, swabbing at his grimy face with an equally grimy bandanna. "How's it goin'?" he called as he approached.

"Can't complain." Nick replaced the gas nozzle in the boot. He pulled out his wallet. "We're interested in seeing Black Bird. Think you could point us in the right direction?"

The young man pursed his lips. "Don't know why anyone'd want to go *there*. To tell you the truth, I don't think there's any way you can make it in that fancy convertible." He turned admiring eyes on the flashy vehicle.

"You're probably right," Nick agreed pleasantly, "but I promised my grandpa I'd give it a try. See, the old guy was a miner. He worked the silver mines there in the early thirties. He made me promise…"

The two men moved out of earshot toward the small station office, Nick talking easily. Cory didn't know whether to admire his chutzpah or condemn the ease with which lies rolled off his tongue. All she could do was sit there sweating, waiting for him to return.

He finally did, climbing into the vehicle and starting the engine. Immediately a blast of hot air hit her in the face; then the air conditioner kicked in.

"So?" she demanded. "Did you get directions?"

"Yep." He drove back out onto the main street.

"That's great."

"That's not great. He's right about the car."

She frowned. "Does that mean we're giving up?"

"Nope. We've just gotta think of another way to get there."

"What? Motorcycles? Helicopter?"

He laughed and it sounded good. He hadn't laughed all day and she found herself smiling in relief.

"Helicopter—now why didn't I think of that? Nope, not a helicopter."

"What, then?"

"Let me put it to you this way. As a Texan, you're probably good with horses."

THREE HOURS LATER, Cory sat astride the tallest horse in the world, while Nick got last-minute directions from an old horse trader who said his name was Slim. If that name had once been more than a joke, he had long since outgrown it. Trying to be charitable, Cory delicately settled on *stout* as a word to describe him.

"Mister," Slim was saying, "I hope to hell you know what you're doin'."

"You and me both." Nick folded the map Slim had drawn and slipped it into his chest pocket.

"You must want to see Black Bird real bad to rent horses and buy all that extra gear and food you loaded on."

"I told you, my grandpa—"

"Yep, your grandpa." Slim walked with Nick to the other horse, the black one. He spared a quick, disapproving glance at Cory. "I can see you handlin' the trip all right, but that wife a'yours don't strike me as pioneer stock."

"Excuse me!" Cory sat up straighter in her saddle, praying that her horse wouldn't take it upon himself to move. "I am *too* pioneer material. I'll make it just fine, thank you very much."

Nick stepped into the stirrup and swung onto the horse's back with a natural grace that made her catch her breath with admiration. He settled into his saddle with such familiarity that she knew he'd told her the truth about his Oklahoma upbringing.

"Don't worry, I'll take care of my wife," he told Slim. He touched his hat brim in a farewell salute. "If we don't have these horses back in a week, come lookin' for us. And bring the law."

Slim cackled with laughter. "Yeah, right, the law. You folks have fun."

"We'll do that." Leaning forward, Nick caught the reins of Cory's horse. "You ready?"

"Absolutely."

"Then hang on!"

He nudged his horse in the ribs and they took off toward the desert at a fast trot, Nick riding like a centaur and Cory barely managing to hang on.

He soon settled the horses into an easy walk. It was too hot to hurry and he had no intention of going on into Black Bird tonight, anyway. Better to arrive in the morning, fresh and wary, instead of late and weary.

Besides, his companion wasn't exactly a cowgirl in spite of her getup. Occasionally he'd glance her way and each time he had to stifle laughter. She clung to that saddle horn like a barnacle to a ship's hull, without apparent thought to style or technique.

But she was game. She didn't complain, although he knew she wasn't having a good ride. She didn't know the half of it. Tomorrow she'd be so sore she'd have trouble walking. But he saw no reason to bring that up now.

They followed the faint trail through the desert until falling dusk made it difficult to discern. When he pulled his horse to a stop, hers did the same. Through gathering darkness, he saw her questioning expression.

"How much farther?" she asked plaintively.

"Only a few more miles. I figure it's not far over that rise."

"Then let's hurry." She clapped her legs against her horse's fat sides; the animal just swung his head around and gave her an insulted glance.

"We're not going in until tomorrow. We have no idea what we'll find, so we're better off spending the night here." He stepped off his horse, tossing the reins over the animal's head.

"But—"

"Shut up, Cory."

Reaching up, he caught her by the waist and lifted her to the ground, resisting the urge to let her body slide along his on its descent. He'd seen her dressed in many different ways, but he thought she looked best of all in the jeans and fancy western shirt, her hat hanging down her back by a stampede string. Her eyes sparkled and she looked alive and glowing, if cross.

But he wasn't going to fall for that. Not again.

He stood her on her feet. "Help me unpack. Then we'll water and grain the horses before we set up camp for the night."

"You mean *here?*" She looked around at miles of sagebrush and shuddered. "Right outdoors in the open?"

"That's what I mean, all right." Tossing a stirrup out of the way, he quickly unsaddled his horse. The black animal was no Pegasus, but he'd been decent enough. Nick laid the saddle on the ground and turned to find her still standing there glaring at him.

"You got a problem?" he asked.

"I…" She licked her lips. "I guess not. It's just that I haven't slept outside since I was a Junior Girl Scout."

"It's easy." He dragged her saddle off the tall sorrel. "Cavemen did it. You can do it."

She lifted her chin. "I know I can. I'm just surprised, that's all. Tell me what you want me to do and I'll do it."

And she did.

SUPPER CONSISTED OF a box of crackers, a can of squirt cheese, a bunch of grapes and water from the canteens. Cory couldn't find it in her heart to call it a tasty meal, yet she enjoyed it enormously.

Alone in a strange desert with a strange, if sexy, man on a strange mission, she found herself happily swept away by the whole thing. As he had pointed out, anything could happen. There could be danger at the end of the trail; there could be danger right here and now.

Glancing at him on the other side of the tiny smokeless fire he'd built out of practically nothing, she quickly pulled her gaze away. Just looking at him sent prickles of excitement through her entire body. Too bad that there could be nothing between them now. Too bad—

"Jeez," he said, "you look like you just swallowed a bug."

"What?" She blinked in confusion.

"You were frowning something fierce."

"I was having fierce thoughts."

He poked at the fire with a stick. "I guess adventure isn't all it's cracked up to be. Adventure can be dirty and uncomfortable and downright difficult."

"I don't care about that," she said impatiently. "You'd be surprised how tough I am."

"That's a comfort."

"Don't you dare laugh at me, Nick Charles!"

"I wouldn't dream of it. Why don't you just lay down with that saddle for a pillow and let me—"

"Let you nothing!"

"Let me give you a little concert." Reaching into the chest pocket of his blue-and-white cowboy shirt, he whipped out a harmonica and held it up with a flourish.

She couldn't help smiling, although she'd sworn she'd give him no further encouragement. "Okay," she said, "but I'm not sure I can actually *lie down*." Shifting even a little bit was painful; every muscle from her waist down screamed for relief.

He watched her with what looked like sympathetic amusement. "Hate to tell you this but you'll feel worse tomorrow. Good thing you're so tough." He played a trill on the harmonica and then launched into "Home on the Range."

Lying there by the campfire with her head on a smooth leather saddle, Cory felt contentment gather around her like a comfortable old quilt. She'd never much cared for harmonica music— who did?—but it was so singularly right for this time and place. Each note seemed to speed straight to the heart she'd vowed to protect.

If only this man was what she'd thought him to be.

If only she'd met him under other circumstances.

If only she didn't...

She pulled her gaze away from him and stared up into the night sky. She spotted one of the dippers, the only constellation she was ever able to identify with any degree of certainty. Following the handle of stars and trying to find the other dipper, she blinked away tears.

Too late she saw the pit into which she'd rushed headlong, for with romance and adventure had come love.

10

NICK STOPPED PLAYING to frown at her, the harmonica held loosely in his hands. "What's wrong?"

She cleared her throat, feeling self-conscious. "Nothing. Why do you ask?"

"You looked a little teary eyed there for a minute. I thought maybe I'd pushed you too far. You know—" he gestured with one arm "—sleeping out and roughing it and all."

"I'm all right with that," she said. "What is it about me that makes people think I can't take a little hardship like everybody else?"

He played a final trill on his harmonica and replaced it in his shirt pocket. "People, as in plural?"

She grimaced. "That guy back there who said I didn't look like a pioneer really annoyed me. It's something my parents would have said. They were so overprotective that sometimes I just wanted to scream. They never wanted me to do *anything.*"

"Mine were just the opposite." Picking up a stick, he poked at the tiny fire. "They wanted me to try everything. When I'd ask if I could do something—you know, swim a river, climb a tree, ride a bronc—my pa would say, 'Think you're big enough?'" Nick's soft laughter sounded affectionate.

"Lucky you. My folks didn't think I was big enough for anything."

"Most kids rebel at that kind of thing."

"I wanted to, but..." She stared into the darkness. "My mother wasn't in the best of health. I felt so terribly guilty about causing her any more grief."

"Only children have it tough."

She nodded. "I always wished I had a sister."

"I had five of 'em, growing up on the family ranch. I think I left home to became a cop in San Francisco because they had me outnumbered."

"Your folks didn't have a problem with you moving so far away?"

He looked surprised. "Why should they? I was an adult."

"I wanted to move to New York City when I graduated from college—this was after my mother died. I wouldn't have dreamed of leaving while she was still alive. Anyway, when my father couldn't talk me out of it, he had a heart attack."

Nick looked startled. "On purpose?"

"No, of course not." She gave him a rueful smile. "At least, I don't think so, but the end result was the same—I was stuck in the same boring life I'd been leading. And I kept on being the same boring person I'd always been."

He looked at her across the fire, a slight smile tugging at his lips. "You, boring? Nah!"

"What you've seen isn't the real me. I'm not a natural blonde."

"Sweetheart," he drawled, "I know that."

The silence sizzled between them. It took a supreme effort for her to look away. "How long were you a policeman?"

"Not long. I got a chance to work for a courier service that delivered sensitive goods, and I jumped at it. The travel appealed to me, more than anything."

"What kind of sensitive goods?"

"All kinds. Diamonds, documents, desperados…"

"A bounty hunter?" She was impressed. She'd never imagined meeting anyone with that kind of background.

"Sometimes. Then a couple of years ago I went to work for Samantha."

"Who is absolutely no relation to you."

"Wrong. She's my boss. That's a pretty heavy relationship."

"But she's not your aunt." Cory gave him a reproachful glance.

He shrugged. "When I'm working, I say and do whatever is necessary to get the job done."

"Lie, cheat, sleep with suspects?"

He let out an exasperated grunt. "You weren't a suspect, not at first, anyway. I didn't get on to you until we were drugged and—"

"Who was drugged?" A chill shot down her spine.

"All of us, so they—whoever they are—could snatch Samantha and Wil." Nick spoke with exaggerated patience, as if explaining to a child…or someone who already knew.

Cory tried to ignore the erratic pounding of her

heart. "Are you telling me that when I woke up in bed with you that night, I wasn't drunk, I was drugged?"

"This is news?"

"You told me I'd had too much to drink and I believed you!"

"Did you? Or did you know better all along?"

She looked at him, so strong and distant and *suspicious* in firelight and moonlight. "It must be awful to go through life not trusting anyone," she said at last, her voice strangled.

"It's safer in my line of work." He stood up and stretched. Taking a few steps, he looked down at her.

"Not to mention lonelier." It was unnerving to have him tower over her, but she refused to flinch.

"Not necessarily." Leaning down, he caught her by the elbows and lifted her to her feet. "Had you ever heard of Samantha Spade or Wil Archer before you met them at La Paloma?"

"No." She met his steady gaze.

"And you have no knowledge whatsoever about the people who took their baby, or whether that baby is alive or dead?"

"No! How could I possibly?"

For a moment, she thought he believed her. Then he seemed to shake away doubts. "Whatever. Com' on, let's go to bed."

"Not together!" She took a quick step back. "I told you, there'll be no more of that. I'm only here to clear my name. You had ulterior motives for sleeping with me before, but how you could think I'd fall for that again…!"

He stood there, outwardly unmoved by her impassioned outburst. He didn't even look disappointed. "I do what I have to do," he said at last. "Untie that blanket off the back of your saddle. These desert nights can get chilly."

So could her heart. Lying next to the embers of the campfire, listening to the lonely howl of a coyote, she squeezed her eyes shut and told herself that she would hate Nick Charles until the day she died.

Yeah, like she hated chocolate.

EVEN A FOUR-WHEEL-DRIVE off-road vehicle would have had difficulty following the route they took the next day to reach Black Bird. And when they got there, all they found was a ragtag collection of crumbling buildings with tumbleweeds rolling down the street in true western-cinema style.

Cory sat carefully atop her tall horse, surveying this depressing scene. Her initial muscle soreness had worn off, but the bone-deep ache remained. And she'd put herself through such torture for *this?*

Nick lifted his reins. "Let's go see if we can find anyone to—"

"Hold it, pilgrims!"

At the command of a strange voice, both Nick and Cory twisted in their saddles to watch a scrawny old man emerge from between two rickety buildings. He dragged a burro behind him, a little creature with packs piled higher than the man's head. Several pickaxes and shovels protruded from the lumpy mass.

Cory caught her breath in dismay. "Oh, the poor little thing! I'm surprised he can walk."

"I walk just fine, lady." The man halted before them, feet spread in a belligerent stance. A floppy, tattered hat rested atop his grizzled head, and his shirtsleeves were rolled up to reveal faded, once-red long johns. Shabby jeans and dirty boots completed the ensemble of a desert prospector.

"Not you. I meant the—"

"I'll do the talkin' here," he said, cutting her off. "State your business in Black Bird."

Nick, who'd been watching with a bemused expression, spoke before Cory could respond. "We're on our honeymoon, old-timer. And you are…?"

The old guy hitched up his jeans. "My handle's Peyote Pete. I'm the law in Black Bird. Also mayor, judge and jury, when they's a need."

"No need as far as we're concerned," Nick said. "Any place around here my wife and I can bed down?"

Peyote Pete scratched his stubbled chin. "Wal, folks by th' name of Jenks over to th' Black Bird Hotel puts folks up now and again. They're a bit peculiar, though, so be sure and tell 'em I sent you."

"We'll do that."

Cory couldn't imagine how Nick kept a straight face. If this old miner called *others* peculiar…

Nick leaned forward with the heels of his hands stacked on the saddle horn. "I'd guess you've been around these parts for a while, Pete."

The old guy's eyes narrowed suspiciously. "What's it to you?"

"We may need directions."

"Nobody knows this neck of the woods like I do," Peyote Pete said with pride. "But if you think I'm gonna let you horn in on my gold mine..." He shook his head vigorously. "No siree-bob, not a chance. You wander around and get yourself lost, it's no skin off my nose, hell, no. Just don't go stickin' *your* nose in my business."

He took off for the opposite side of the street. "Come along, Dingus," he yelled at the donkey. The little animal heaved what could only be a sigh and ambled after his retreating master.

Nick tipped his hat and called, "Nice meeting you, Pete. Maybe we'll see you again before we—"

"Harrumph!" Pete waved off further pleasantries and disappeared between two tipsy buildings.

For a few seconds, Cory and Nick sat in silence. Then she asked incredulously, "Is that guy for real?"

Nick lifted his reins. "Your guess is as good as mine. I have a feeling we'll find out before this is over, though."

Cory did, too.

A WEATHERED SIGN dangled from a single chain across the front of a shabby, two-story brick building: Black Bird Hotel, Purveyor of Fine Spirits and Good Food, Jim Jenks, Prop.

"Jim Jenks, Prop." had been added freehand with a paintbrush.

Cory groaned. "This is getting ridiculous," she announced. "I'm not going inside a place like that, let alone sleep there. It looks like it'll come crashing down any minute."

"Suit yourself." Nick swung out the saddle and tossed his reins over the wheel of a dilapidated wagon, amused by her show of defiance. Turning away, he stepped up onto the decaying boardwalk.

He heard her scramble after him but he didn't slow down, just pushed through a surprisingly sturdy door and entered the lobby. To the left he could see a dark bar and straight ahead a registration desk, all of it thick with dust. He sneezed and a puff of grime rose from a nearby wall hanging. Dust motes danced on rays of sunshine shafting across a carpet so old and threadbare that its original color would forever remain in doubt.

The place was like a tomb: no people noises, no gambling noises.

Cory ran up his heels and he uttered an annoyed exclamation.

"Sorry," she whispered, hanging on to his shoulders. He felt her cheek against his back as she pressed closer. "This place is spooky. Maybe there really are ghosts in ghost towns."

"Who you callin' a ghost, missy?"

The unexpectedly hoarse voice of a woman made Cory shriek and press more tightly against Nick. If he had to take sudden action, they'd be doomed. He should tell her to back off, but she felt so damn good with her breasts pressed against him and her arms circling his waist.

He said in his most pleasant tone, "Mrs. Jenks, I presume?"

She came around the registration desk and he saw that she was dressed just like Peyote Pete. She was considerably bigger than the old prospector, though: perhaps six feet tall and broad through the shoulders. She wore her stringy gray hair pulled up in a loose knot on top of her head.

"That's right, Marge Jenks." She eyed them cautiously. "Somethin' you want?"

"Indeed there is." When Nick walked forward, Cory shuffled along behind him without releasing her grip on his waist. "Peyote Pete sent us. We'd like a room for the night."

"Two rooms!" Cory peered around his shoulder.

"If you have two," Nick agreed graciously. "But if you only have one—"

"I got two, if I decide to let you have 'em." Marge Jenks squinted at them. "We don't get many tourists in Black Bird. What brings you here, stranger?"

"A search for privacy, Miz Jenks. I'm on my honeymoon. You see, my wife and I—"

"You two are married?" Marge Jenks demanded, cutting in. "If she's your bride, why does she want a room of her own?"

"Because she's mad at me, ma'am. She doesn't like horses and I told her it would only take an hour to ride here from Cairo. We ended up sleeping out last night and that really ticked her off. She'll get over it, though. She loves me."

Mrs. Jenks smiled suddenly, almost flirtatiously. "Good-lookin' fella like you, I can believe it," she said heartily. "Sure, I got rooms for you. Just sign here." Walking back behind the counter, she twirled the huge registration book toward them on a turntable. Again, dust rose.

Nick took the pen she offered. "Anyone else staying here at the present?"

"Nope. We had us a young antropo—anthropolog—anthro—"

"Anthropologist?"

"That's right, a student. He checked out day before last."

"Where does Peyote Pete live?"

Mrs. Jenks laughed heartily. "That old faker? Who knows! Maybe he's livin' at that Black Bird Mine of his."

"Anyone else in town?"

"Not nary a one, except for Mr. Jenks, of course. It's been real quiet here this summer, and that's how me'n Mr. Jenks likes it." She twirled the book back around and glanced at the name. "Okay, Mr. and Miz Charles, I'll put you in 120C and 635."

Cory seemed to find her voice. "But there are only two floors. How can you have a 6—"

"Mind your tongue, young woman." Mrs. Jenks scowled. "I didn't number them rooms. If you don't like it, you can lump it."

"Yes, ma'am."

Nick had never heard that deferential tone in Cory's voice before. Maybe she'd assessed the situation and realized that she needed Mrs. Jenks's goodwill. He gave the woman his most winsome smile. "Can we get our meals from you, too, Mrs. Jenks?"

"That'll be extra."

"Of course."

"And you gotta be on time. We eat at six, twelve and six—no ifs, ands or buts."

"Six *a.m.?*" Cory blurted.

"One'a them sixes is," Mrs. Jenks agreed. "Okay, that's a hundred bucks a night for the rooms—"

Cory let out an incredulous snort, then tried to pretend she was just clearing her throat.

"—Plus another fifty for meals—"

"Sounds fair," Nick agreed.

"In advance."

He pulled out his wallet.

"Each!"

He laughed. "Don't you think that's carrying highway robbery a bit far?"

She snickered. "Can't blame me for tryin'. That'll be a hundred and fifty smackers right up front—cash on the barrel head."

He counted out the bills and she took them with a sigh of pleasure. Fishing beneath the counter, she pulled up two big, old-fashioned keys and offered them.

Nick balanced both keys on one palm. "We'll go upstairs and take a look around before we bring our stuff in from the horses," he decided. "Which room do you want, Cory?"

Mrs. Jenks leaned over the counter, a sly grin on her broad face. "Give her 635," she suggested.

"Okay." He handed over that key. "Why?"

Mrs. Jenks laughed. "Because it's haunted, is why. This ain't called a ghost town for nothin'." She broke into raucous peals of laughter.

Cory looked down at the key on her palm and then very carefully laid it back on the counter. "Thanks all the same, but I don't think I'm quite as angry at my husband as I thought I was," she said. "Shall we go up now, *sweetheart?*"

CORY GLARED AT THE NARROW bed on its wrought-iron frame. How did people *sleep* on these things? The bed was not only too small, it also looked lumpy, and the pillows were flat as pancakes.

"This is impossible," she announced.

Nick glanced around from the tall, narrow window from which vantage point he'd been surveying the empty street. He let the heavy velvet draperies fall back into place, and the inevitable cloud of dust enveloped the room. "What's impossible?"

"That bed." She widened her horizons. "This room."

"Ever hear the one about beggars and choosers?"

She sighed. He was right, although she hated to admit it. "It's bound to be better than sleeping outdoors," she argued rhetorically, "isn't it?"

He shrugged. "I don't plan to do much sleeping, anyway."

"Because you'll be snooping around looking for Samantha?"

"Because being cooped up with you in a tiny room with one tiny bed between us and orders to keep hands off isn't conducive to rest."

"Oh!" she said softly, his frankness taking her aback. Maybe he'd had other reasons to make love to her than a simple quest for information. Maybe—

The clanging of a bell cut off further perusal of that possibility, followed by Mrs. Jenks's raucous call: "Soup's on! Come get it or I'll throw it to the dogs!"

Nick and Cory exchanged glances. Then he reached out and tilted her chin so he could gaze into her face.

"Look," he said, "we want Mrs. Jenks to keep on thinking we're on our honeymoon. We won't be able to do that if you keep scowling and bitching and kicking up a fuss."

Cory sucked in a quick indignant breath and just as quickly let it out again. "You're right," she moaned. "I'm not usually so bitchy. I just feel as if somebody else is pulling my strings, you know? I feel so…out of control."

"I do, too, in a way. But we've got to play this game, Cory. Samantha and Wil are close, I feel it in my bones. After lunch we'll start checking out the town. If that doesn't pan out we'll start on the surrounding countryside. If they're here, we'll find them."

She nodded slowly. "If they're here." But in her heart, she wasn't even sure they'd actually been kidnapped. It all seemed so far-fetched. Maybe this was some kind of wild-goose chase.

But she wouldn't tell Nick her suspicions. She wouldn't tell Nick anything, ever again.

MR. JENKS APPEARED for lunch and turned out to be a shorter, thinner version of his wife. He didn't seem at all surprised to see company at the table, nor did he seem surprised that lunch consisted of cheese sandwiches on stale white bread and canned fruit cocktail.

He ate quickly, smiled vaguely and departed.

Mrs. Jenks looked after him with a fond expression. "He's writing a book," she confided, "a very important book about nuclear fission. He's a genius, you know."

Nick didn't, but wasn't surprised to hear it. He dropped his bread crust on the chipped white plate and smiled at his landlady. "We plan to explore Black Bird this afternoon," he said. "Anything we should know—any dangers, I mean? Walls about to fall down, sinkholes, roofs on the verge of collapse?"

"Yep, some'a all them things. Best advice is be careful." She scowled. "And don't be late for supper."

"Six o'clock," Cory said quickly. "Shall we go, *darling?*"

"By all means, *angel.*"

They walked out of the hotel dining room hand in hand.

Once outside, Cory flounced away from him. "Enough's enough," she complained. "There's nobody around to—"

Peyote Pete ambled around the corner of the hotel, dragging Dingus behind him. "You folks still here? I thought you'd have what you come for and be gone by now."

Cory shot into Nick's arms as if propelled by a cannon. Nick was starting to like this aspect of their masquerade.

"We decided to put up at Black Bird's picturesque hotel," he said. "Would you like to show us around?"

"Hell, no!" The man turned away. "How long you say you're plannin' to stay?"

"A few days, maybe more. Maybe less. Depends."

"On what?" Pete's eyes gleamed with curiosity.

"On whether my wife enjoys being alone with me as much as I enjoy being alone with her." Okay, that was laying it on thick, but it was for a noble cause.

Cory patted his cheek, but he could see her gritted teeth. "Sweetheart, you know there's nothing I like more than being alone with my big, handsome husband."

Pete harrumphed. "You two could make a man sick t' his stomach," he declared. "Me and Dingus can't stand much more of this."

While he dragged the stiff-legged little animal away, Cory whispered to Nick, "And neither can I!"

THE BOOMTOWN of Black Bird had had it all at one time—not only a hotel but several saloons, a number of false-fronted stores, even a bank and a church. Structures were mostly of wood, although there were a few of brick and stone. The wooden buildings had suffered greatly from the passage of time. Nick refused to let Cory enter most of them.

One they did go into was the Dash-It-All Saloon, and it was like stepping back in time. Dusty bottles that once held liquor still fronted the cracked and crazed mirror behind the bar. At one end, two small glasses marked the spot where perhaps the last drink had been served.

Rummaging around behind the bar, Cory pulled out a newspaper from beneath a tray of glasses. Laying the paper on the bar, she opened it carefully. Her soft, appreciative "Oh!" had Nick swinging toward her.

"What have you got there?" He walked over to see.

Her smile was brilliant as she held up a fluffy feather—marabou, he would guess if put to the test.

She waved it through the air languidly. "Isn't this fabulous? Who do you suppose it belonged to?"

He enjoyed her enthusiasm. "Probably some dance-hall queen named Belle."

"Or maybe named Corinne." She poked the tapered end of the feather into her hair, weaving it in and out of the blond curls to hold it in place. "How do I look? Do you think I could have gotten a job here?" Cocking her head, she gave him a saucy smile.

"Cory," he said with heartfelt sincerity, "as far as I'm concerned, you could've got a job anywhere you wanted—and still can."

She snatched the feather from her hair. "I wish I had your confidence."

"I've got confidence to spare." He crooked his finger at her. "Come over here and find out."

"I…" She wavered; he saw it in her face, in the way her body strained toward him without actually moving at all. She drew back sharply.

"You're wasting your time. There's nothing I can tell you."

He watched her walk out past the front doors with the broken hinges, thinking that there was plenty she could tell him, if she only would.

And it wasn't all about Samantha and Laura, either.

THAT NIGHT THEY FELL asleep side by side, lying rigidly on the too-small bed. Nick woke up the following morning with a raging hard-on and Cory in his arms.

Ripping himself from the scene of sweet temptation, he stumbled down the hall to the bathroom with its hanging water closet and rusty claw-footed tub. Staring into the cracked mirror over the stained and chipped sink, he grimaced at the bloodshot eyes and the bristled jaw, but knew that his biggest problem wasn't anything visible.

His biggest problem was his concentration, which stank. He had to keep his mind on business. So far he hadn't seen the first thing to indicate Samantha and Wil had ever been anywhere near Black Bird, Nevada. Nick was just going through the motions, because in reality, Corinne Leblanc was driving him nuts.

Was that coincidence or premeditation?

He groaned and his shoulders sagged. The room with the ghost was looking better and better.

11

FOR TWO DAYS, Nick and Cory searched the ghost town with methodical thoroughness, going in and out of every building he judged safe. They took their meals with the Jenkses, Spartan offerings with little to recommend them. Cory could tell she was losing weight, which she figured was just about the only good thing going on in Black Bird.

Generators powered lights in the lobby and the Jenkses' private quarters, while "guests" made do with kerosene lamps. This made the lobby the logical gathering place after nightfall. By the second evening, Cory was a mass of nerves. A bit of hand laundry done in Marge's tin tub with a washboard failed to distract her for long. When she settled down in the lobby with the Jenkses' amazing collection of *Reader's Digest* condensed novels, she found herself paying more attention to Nick than to words on the page.

He sat clear across the room from her, at a poker table that seemed incongruously out of place. He'd spread maps across the tattered green felt surface, including several unearthed in the remains of the assayer's office. How she envied his concentration!

Her own was chaotic, and impatient with herself, she fidgeted until nine-thirty, then rose abruptly. "I'm going up now," she announced, "but there's no need for you to—"

"Yeah, there is. We gotta talk." He shoved the maps aside and stood up. "I'll come with you." The expression on his face was not encouraging.

As soon as they were inside their room, Nick made an announcement.

"Tomorrow's the deadline," he said, wishing she didn't look quite so delectable sitting there on the side of the bed examining fingernails chipped from digging around in the ruins. Behind her hung the laundry she'd washed out earlier, slung across a rope hanging between gaslight fixtures that no longer worked.

"Uh-oh," she said. "Deadline for what?"

"Us. If we haven't found anything by the end of the day and haven't received further instructions, we're getting out of here."

She met his gaze with a kind of natural innocence. No makeup, no artifice at all now, just gorgeous woman. "But why?" she asked plaintively. "Where else can we look?"

"*We* can't look anywhere else. You're going home to Texas and I'm going to the police."

"But, Nick, you said—"

"I don't care what I said. This is what I'm saying now." He spoke roughly because he realized more every day how much he was going to hate to see her go. Of course, if she turned out to be Laura Spade-Archer...

He shook off that prospect and all its uncertainties. He'd tried and failed to get through to Joel earlier in the day with the Jenkses' shortwave radio, so there was nothing he could do on that score.

She frowned. "I don't get it."

"You don't have to get it." What was there to get? That they were wasting their time? Besides, she was driving him crazy. If he had to spend one more night in this room with her…

He snatched up a lamp. "I'm sleeping in 635," he announced. "I'll see you tomorrow at breakfast."

"But—"

"Good night, Cory. Pleasant dreams." He couldn't get out of there fast enough.

THEY SPENT WHAT WAS TO BE their final day in Black Bird circling the town systematically on horseback, each swoop larger than the next. All Nick found was the trail of Peyote Pete and Dingus, which he eventually decided to follow— Cory supposed out of sheer desperation, since they'd had any number of conversations with the eccentric old man already.

The trail led up across rocky, sage-covered hills. After an hour or so, Nick pointed to a stand of cottonwoods ahead.

"Water," he said. "Must be the oasis the guy in Cairo mentioned."

Cory shoved sweat-dampened hair back under her hat and licked dry lips. "I sure hope so. I'm melting. A swim is exactly what I need."

"Forget it. Marge said Pete's Black Bird Mine is north of the springs, and that's where his tracks are headed. I want to take a look."

"I think we should take a swim and *then* take a look."

"We don't have time," Nick said impatiently.

"Then we'll just have to make time!" She felt steam rising from her damp face and neck. "Water! I can't possibly pass it by."

Stiff in their saddles, they glared at each other. Then he spun his back to the left.

"I'm going to that mine."

"Great," she called after him. "Have a good time and pick me up on the way back!"

Kicking her horse in the sides, she urged him up the grade toward the trees. She hated to be stubborn, but the mere possibility that there might be enough water for her to take a dip was more than she could resist. At the very least, there'd be shade. That beckoning oasis would be paradise, with Nick or without him.

Then she heard his horse's hooves behind her and acknowledged to herself that "with him" would be better.

CORY FLOATED ON HER BACK and looked up through the leafy canopy at a blazing blue dome. A redheaded bird took sudden flight and she watched its colors blend into the sky.

She hadn't felt this content since they'd left Las Vegas. Turning her head, she saw Nick standing in waist-deep water watching her, looking so strong and gorgeous that she wanted to swim right up to him and drag him under for a quick—

She flopped over on her belly and took a few strokes before standing up. The deepest part of this desert pool couldn't be more than four feet, but it was glorious nonetheless. She hadn't even hesitated before stripping down to her undies and plunging in.

She assumed Nick had done likewise, until he turned and walked out of the water and she saw his backside, pale where a swimsuit normally covered it. She gulped. He was perfectly naked. Perfectly...

And what was he doing? He seemed to be...arranging their discarded clothing into a pallet beneath the shade of a cottonwood. When he turned and crooked his forefinger at her, she didn't ask why. She didn't have to; he reminded her of a flag unfurled. Talk about a private eyeful!

For a moment she stood stock-still in the water, completely mesmerized. Then she walked toward him as if reeled in on a line, straight out of the water and into his arms.

She knew she shouldn't do this. She'd vowed never to succumb to him again. If she did, she knew it would be even harder to walk away tomorrow.

But if she didn't, she'd never be able to forgive herself. She reached for him as he reached for her and they came together in a crushing embrace. Mouths sought and found; bodies melded. Holding the kiss, they sank onto their knees on the makeshift bed he'd so carefully arranged, then tumbled over onto their sides. Legs tangled while the kiss went on and on. She reveled in his desire for her, and hers for him.

They were so perfectly matched in so many ways—all the ways that counted, except for one:

trust. Still, she let him whisk aside her soggy un-dies and join his body with hers, then carry her along to a quick, intense fulfillment.

Lying there replete, she turned her head away to hide damp eyes. Leaving him tomorrow would be hell. And she hadn't even managed to clear her name.

He stroked the small birthmark below her nip-ple. "Thank you," he murmured into her ear.

She shivered. "For what?"

"For letting me love you."

She groaned at his choice of words. "It was sex, not love."

"You're sure of that?"

"You couldn't love a woman you don't trust."

"Maybe I've changed my mind about you." He gave her a lopsided grin. "I did have plenty of time to think last night."

"Maybe? Maybe! You can stop trying to make me feel better about what just happened." She sat up, but refused to look at him. "I don't blame you, Nick. You don't have to sweet-talk me after the fact."

He ran the tips of his fingers down her naked spine. She caught her breath, arching away from his touch.

"It's not sweet talk," he said. "I finally listened to my gut and—"

"Your *gut?*"

"Gut, heart, whatever you want to call it. I've gotten to know you since we left Las Vegas. Mata Hari herself couldn't have fooled me for this long. You said you didn't know anything and I'm starting to suspect you know even less than you think."

"What's that supposed to mean? Are you keeping something from me that I should—" She broke off, frowning at the sandy ground beside the makeshift pallet.

"What is it?" He scooted over beside her, instantly on the alert. "What have you found?"

"Some really strange tracks." Holding her breath, she touched one of the deep puncture holes in the earth. Lifting her gaze to his, she waited for him to confirm what she suspected.

His eyes narrowed and then he smiled ever so slowly. "At last."

"You mean…?"

"I mean that's the track of the high-heeled Samantha-bird. Get dressed, sweetheart. We've finally got a clue."

CORY HUNKERED DOWN among the boulders, clinging to Nick's arm and staring at the entrance to the Black Bird Mine. The sign was so faded that she could barely make out the letters. A rock slide had partially blocked the entrance into the side of the hill, but it was the Black Bird, all right.

She was so excited that she breathed in shallow pants. "I don't get it," she whispered. "I thought you said the mine was north of here."

"Yeah. That's apparently what Pete wanted everybody to think." Nick gave her a wry glance. "If you hadn't got stubborn on me, chances are we'd never have found it."

"Me, stubborn?" She laughed, keeping it low,

then added more seriously, "Do you think they're in there?"

"I'd bet on it."

"Then what are we waiting for?"

He held her back. "Let's get the lay of the land before we charge in and get someone hurt." He pulled the pistol from his waistband and checked it; a grunt of approval said everything was in order.

"Nick, do you think—"

"Shh. Someone's coming."

Peyote Pete appeared around an outcropping of rock. This time the old miner rode Dingus instead of dragging him, and he kicked the little burro in the ribs unmercifully with every step. At the entrance to the mine, Pete jumped off with surprising agility. With a quick glance around, he clambered over the rocks and disappeared inside.

Nick let out his breath in a satisfied grunt. "Okay," he said, "let's go. But stay behind me. There's bound to be trouble."

Cory wasn't about to argue. He was no stranger to danger, but to her, the situation was terrifying—in a very exciting way, of course. Adventure! She couldn't wait to tell Crystal.

They scrambled down off the rocks and followed Pete into the cavern. The dank smell of wet earth assailed her nostrils, and the temperature dropped dramatically with every step. Within ten feet, the tunnel snaked to the left, becoming dark as a tomb. Quickly disoriented, she clung to Nick's belt loops and trusted that he knew what he was doing.

They hadn't gone much farther when she heard

the low murmur of voices ahead. Rounding another curve, she saw light. When Nick pressed against the wall, she followed his lead. Carefully they inched forward until they stood next to an opening off the main tunnel.

Peyote Pete's gravelly voice came to her. "So how do you like them apples, Sammy-girl? I got you just where I always wanted you."

Wil answered, not Samantha. "Leave her alone! Don't you think you've done enough to her? You're not even human to—"

"She's the one who ain't human, never was. Snotty, snooty, and can't even see what's right under her eyes. Never could, never will. Heh-heh-heh!"

Sam's strident voice cut through Pete's maniacal chortles. "You said we could see her. You promised."

"I told you she's comin'."

"You've been telling us that for days. Why should we believe you?"

"Because you ain't got a choice."

Samantha groaned. "You can't keep us chained to this wall forever."

"I'll unchain you long enough to write that check."

Wil's voice broke in. "And then what? You can't afford to let us go."

The silence stretched on and on. Finally Pete said, "I got that all figured out." And he didn't sound crazy any longer, just scary.

Shaking off Cory's grip, Nick peered cautiously around the opening, then stepped into the entryway of the subterranean cavern. Peeking around the wall into the chamber, Cory saw Pete standing with his back toward the entry, while Samantha and Wil slumped against the far wall, only about ten feet away. Their arms were raised above their heads, their wrists shackled to the rock wall with iron bracelets. They saw the newcomers before Pete was aware of their presence, but didn't give anything away beyond the merest flicker of an eye.

Stepping up behind Pete with stealthy agility, Nick clamped an arm around the old guy's neck. Into the startled man's ear, he growled, "That was easy. It'll be harder to keep from snapping your scrawny neck like a dried twig, you old degenerate."

Cory grabbed Nick's elbow, uttering sharply, "No, don't!" She had no sympathy for what Pete had done, but Nick looked angry enough to make good his threat.

With an unwilling grunt, Nick let up the pressure on the guy's throat slightly. "Okay, but somebody better tell me what the hell's going on here."

Samantha straightened against the wall. "What took you so long?" she screeched. "If you think it's fun sitting around in a hole in the ground with a maniac occasionally waving a gun in your face—"

"Hold that thought," Nick said, cutting her off. "Cory, can you figure out how to get them loose?"

She glanced around the grotto. "Where's the key?"

"On the hook by the door." Wil pointed with

his chin. "Could you hurry? My arms feel like they're ready to fall off."

While Cory scurried to free them, Samantha slumped back against the wall. She looked, Cory thought, like she'd been through the mill. She wore a miner's overalls, a ragged, red plaid work shirt—and the high heels that might have saved her life. Her hair straggled around a face with no trace of makeup, not even the trademark red lipstick.

She might be bloody, figuratively speaking, but she was unbowed. Her amber eyes flashed. "That lollipop you're holding," she said contemptuously to Nick, "is Peter Archer, my ex-brother-in-law."

"The one you said was dead?"

"That's what he wanted us to think," Wil explained grimly. "As you can plainly see, he's gone completely around the bend. He's always been the black sheep of the Archer family, but I didn't think even *he* could stoop so low."

Nick's arm tightened across Pete's Adam's apple. "And his motive was…?"

Samantha's lip curled. "Money and revenge— the classic twosome. Even though Peter was older, he was completely wild and unpredictable. After he stole their mother's jewels, their father had the good sense to cut him off without a dime."

"Then why didn't you get a ransom note?"

"Because he got money from someone else."

Cory's hands froze on the rusty lock into which she struggled to insert an equally rusty key. "He sold your baby?"

Samantha gave the younger woman a faintly hostile glance. "In a word, yes. He never intended to return our child. He got the money from a bird named Mark something-or-other, a badass with mob ties. It was no big deal to Peter, what happened to the baby. He just wanted to come out of it with a little money and a lot of revenge."

Pete finally got enough air to squawk. "Yeah, and I did, too, you—!"

Nick readjusted his grip and Pete subsided with an abundance of unpleasant gurgles. "Is this Mark still involved?"

"Up to his ass. He's the one who doped us and got his pals to sneak us out of La Paloma." Samantha, arms finally free, rubbed bruised wrists without wincing or betraying any sign of discomfort. "That's Peter's story, anyway. I don't know that I believe him entirely, he's such a lying piece of trash."

"Sticks and stones," Peter yelled. "Heh-heh-heh!"

Nick shoved the old miner up against the wall, holding on to him by an arm twisted behind his back. "Are you two all right, then?" he asked Samantha and Will. "Did he hurt you?"

Samantha sneered. "Beyond forced marches in the desert? Besides being filthy and hungry and chained up like animals? Besides spending hours on end with a madman talking in riddles?"

Pete cackled. "The answer to the riddle is right under your noses," he howled with fiendish glee.

Samantha clenched her hands into fists. "I'd like to work on *your* nose."

"What about the baby?" Cory couldn't keep

quiet any longer. "Did he tell you what happened to Laura?"

Genuine pain twisted Samantha's face. "All he'll say is that she's alive and he can produce her—for a million dollars."

"Cheap at twice the price," Pete burbled. "Gotta get my mine up and runnin', don'cha know? Besides, you'n my little brother owe me."

"Then produce her," Wil snarled, "and I'll write the check—just before I kill you with my bare hands."

"You'll have to beat me to him." Samantha lunged to her feet, a feral gleam in her eyes, and launched herself toward her mortal enemy.

"Damn it, don't—!" Nick tried to fend her off, but she'd caught him flat-footed. Nor did she have the slightest compunction about pummeling him with elbows and shoulders to get at the object of her hatred. Forced to release Pete, Nick made a grab for her, but she ducked and somehow managed to clip him squarely beneath the chin with the top of her head.

He staggered back. Pete yelped with glee and fumbled in his coat pocket, hauling out an enormous pistol.

"Hands up!" He waved the weapon around until he had everyone's attention. "You, big guy, pull that pistol outa your pants and drop it real easy like."

Nick grabbed Samantha's waist to keep her from attacking again. A thin trail of blood trickled from one corner of his mouth and he licked it away. "Damn it," he roared, "of all the lame-brained—"

"Who you callin' names?" Pete shrilled.

"Her, who d'ya think?" Nick shoved Samantha toward Wil, along with a warning glance. Pulling out his pistol using only thumb and forefinger, he placed it carefully on the ground. "Can't we talk this over?" he asked Pete with a placating smile.

"What's your bargaining chip?" Pete looked interested, if suspicious. "Remember, money talks."

"Money won't do you any good because you'll never get away with this."

"Heh-heh-heh!" Pete waved the pistol again and everyone it passed automatically ducked. "I been gettin' away with it for mor'n twenty-five years."

Nick nodded. "That was the perfect crime, all right, but now too many people know about it. Why don't you give me the gun and we'll work something out."

"I ain't givin' you no gun." Pete's eyes narrowed. "And I don't see we got anything to work out. My brother's gonna write me a nice fat check and then…" He blinked as if suddenly confused. "I had a plan," he mumbled.

"I think your plan is to turn us loose," Nick urged. "If you do, we can see you get the help you need to—"

"You *are* callin' me crazy!" The pistol carved a wandering slash through the air until it pointed straight at Nick's broad chest. "I don't like that kinda talk."

Watching in horror, Cory thought she could actually see the grimy forefinger tighten around the trigger. Without thinking of the consequences, she screamed and flung herself between Nick and the man holding the gun.

Nick grabbed her and swung her around roughly, protecting her with his body. An explosion rocked the small chamber and rock splinters flew past her cheek.

Nick froze, holding her so tight she could barely breathe. "Are you all right?"

"Yes. What about you?" She tried to fight free of his embrace so she could see if he'd been hurt. "Oh, God, Nick, if anything happens to you—"

"Cory?" A new voice cut through the confusion. "Is that you?"

Satisfied Nick was all right, Cory twisted around to stare at the curly haired man standing in the entryway, brandishing a pistol of his own. Unlike Pete, he looked as if he knew how to use it. Her eyes widened in surprise. "Uncle Mario?"

"I've been expecting you, Mark." That was Wil. "Did you bring our little girl?"

"Laura!" Samantha covered her mouth with her hands, looking as if she might faint. Her frantic gaze sought assurance from the newcomer. "Oh, God, where is she?"

"Shut up, all of you." Mark-Mario's glare included the entire room before turning on his partner in crime. "Pete, you son of a bitch, drop that gun or I'll fill you so full of lead you'll look like Swiss cheese."

Pete's jaw dropped, and so did his weapon. Apparently satisfied, Mario's attention shifted to Nick. "You—! I had her stashed away safe at La Paloma, but you had to drag her into this mess."

Nick raised his empty hands in a gesture of innocence. "Hey, I was just following orders."

"That was me!" Pete chortled. "I was hangin' around, making sure you took the bait I planted on her. Took you long enough to find it!"

Mario bared his teeth in a snarl. "I don't give a damn about any of that. I'm taking her out of here and nobody better get in our way." His angry gaze touched Cory and softened. "Com' on, sweetheart," he coaxed. "We're getting out of this mess while we still can."

Cory stared at the man, but made no move to go to him. "First tell me what's going on, Uncle Mario. I've been looking everywhere for you. I never expected to find you *here*."

Samantha took a staggering step forward, her face ghastly pale. "My God," she whispered, "can it be true? Can this be…Laura?"

"Hell's bells!" A wild-eyed Peyote Pete flung himself toward the entry. "Head for the hills, the dam has busted!"

He smacked into the gunman so hard and so unexpectedly that Mario grunted and went down, taking the smaller man with him. With a snarl of rage, Nick sprang, yanking Pete aside and planting one cowboy boot firmly on Mario's gun hand. Retrieving the weapon, Nick rolled the man over onto his stomach and jabbed a knee none too gently in the middle of his back.

Wil grabbed his brother and shoved him up against the wall again, hard. Then he, like everyone else in the room, looked at Cory.

Who just stood there at a complete loss. Samantha took a step forward, her hands lifting in entreaty and her face naked in its vulnerability.

Cory flinched and took a step back—because finally, she understood. "Wait a minute," she begged in a strangled voice, "I'm not who—you can't believe—*I'm* not Laura!" She broke off, on the fringes of a panic attack. This was crazy, and yet...

Nick scooped his pistol from the floor and climbed off Mario's back. He held out a hand to Cory. "Steady," he said. "We're about to clear your name, just like you wanted."

She gave him a quick, confused glance. What was he talking about? She couldn't possibly be the Archer baby. She'd grown up knowing who she was, who her parents were—but Uncle Mario's presence threw everything in doubt.

Samantha drew a shaky breath. "I've dreamed of this day ever since my baby was taken."

"Stop saying that! How many times do I have to tell you that I'm not your baby?"

Samantha didn't waver. Her gaze trapped Cory's. "My baby had a small—"

"I don't even like you," Cory cried, helpless before Samantha's utter conviction. "You don't even like *me*."

"If you're my Laura, I'll *love* you," Samantha snapped. "Shut up and listen! My baby has a small lightning-shaped mark just below her left—"

Cory gasped and stumbled back into Nick's arms. She couldn't seem to catch her breath, so he spoke for her.

"Cory has a small lightning-shaped mark just below her left—"

"Damn it, Nicholas!" Samantha hauled back as if prepared to punch him out. Her eyes glittered dangerously. "Where the hell do you get off checking out my daughter's left—"

"I've had ample opportunity, Samantha. You encouraged me, in case it's slipped your mind. You said I should…"

Their words faded to a din while Cory tried to cope with the knowledge that Nick knew what was going on, Uncle Mario knew what was going on, everybody here, with one exception, knew what was going on.

At which point, the only one who *didn't* know what was going on sank gently to the floor in a dead faint.

12

A TENSE GROUP of four men and two women entered the Black Bird Hotel two hours later. Everyone was subdued, but none more so than Cory.

Nick was worried about her. She didn't seem to be functioning on all cylinders, as if the shock had been too great. When he'd tried to talk to her, she'd turned her back. Nor would she speak to Samantha. Finally everyone just left her alone, although this didn't appear to be any easier on them than it was on him.

Marge Jenks met them in the lobby, her normal self-possession in shreds. "The state cops are on their way here," she announced. "They called and so did a guy named Joe…Joe Castor?"

Samantha gasped. "Joel called? What did he say?"

Marge frowned. "He didn't call you, whoever you are. He called Nick."

"It's all right, Marge." Nick patted her hand, keeping a watchful eye on Cory. She didn't look as if she was even following the conversation. "Just give me the message."

"Right." She took a breath and reached deep into her memory. "He said he heard from San…San Diego—"

"San Francisco."

"—and you were right about the footprints."

"Fingerprints."

Samantha looked on the verge of exploding. "What fingerprints? What have you done, Nicholas?"

He held up a hand to calm her, but spoke to Marge. "What else did he say? Did he mention Laura?"

Marge frowned. "Now that you mention it— but I thought he said Nora. That shortwave gets a real bad connection sometimes. He said the prints on the glass were Laura's. I'm sure that's it."

Any remaining doubts had just been shattered, but Cory hadn't hung around to hear. She sat alone in a stiff-backed chair on the far side of the room, elbows propped on her knees and her head in her hands. Sunlight shafted off her golden hair, more tangles now than curls, but still the most beautiful hair Nick had ever seen.

And the most beautiful woman, the woman he loved. That realization settled in the pit of his stomach like a brick in a bubble bath. What was she thinking? What was she feeling?

Samantha let out a soft moan. "Oh, God, I knew it was true. Nick, you had them match up Cory's prints with the ones they got of Laura during the investigation, didn't you."

"Yeah, and I had them match both those to Cory's birth certificate, or I should say, the real Corinne Leblanc's birth certificate. Sounds as if Joel put it all together and decided on his own to call the law."

Samantha hardly seemed to be listening. With soul-deep yearning in her eyes, she stared across the room at Cory, motionless in the chair. Wil, holding a gun on the two trussed bad men, looked equally shaken.

Samantha whipped around to glare at Nick. "Do something!" she commanded. "She's *got* to listen to us now."

Nick felt a surge of anger so strong that it surprised him, followed by an overwhelming desire to protect Cory. "Back off, Sam," he growled. "This is a lot for her to take in."

Mark-Mario, hands tied behind his back, edged closer. "Let me talk to her," he pleaded. "I owe her that."

Nick hesitated, then nodded abruptly. "Yeah, you do owe her, after the way you messed up her life. For that matter, all of us owe her. But if you say anything to make her feel worse—"

"Who, me?" Mario looked offended. "I've known her longer than any of you. I'm her uncle. I love her."

Samantha's fingers curved into claws and she let out a low growl that made the hair stand up on the back of Nick's neck.

Nick made a quick decision. "Wil, tie your brother to that pillar over there and join us. I'll be responsible for this one."

Grabbing Mario by the lapel of his flashy silk shirt, Nick dragged him over to stand before Cory. She looked up with eyes that barely seemed to focus.

"It isn't true, is it, Uncle Mario? My mother was Rhea Moretti Leblanc, not…" she shot a hostile glance at Samantha "…*her*."

"Honey…" Mario sank to his knees before her,

his arms bound awkwardly behind his back. "Rhea loved you and raised you. She was your mother in every way but one."

"Oh, God." Cory closed her eyes. She looked completely bewildered.

Mario continued relentlessly. "When Rhea's baby died, she just plain went crazy. I think it was that sudden infant thing, it happened so fast and was so unexpected. She wouldn't even let me call the doctor, and when I said I was going to anyway she tried to cut her wrists." His face twisted with remembered anguish. "You know how sensitive she was."

"Yes, but… It wouldn't be possible just to switch one baby for another, would it?" Cory looked around wildly for support.

"I don't know what's usual," Mario said, "but I know how *we* did it. Pete wanted to get even with his brother and make a couple of bucks in the process. When he snatched their kid, the timing was just right. I gave him a place to put it—put you. I borrowed fifty thousand bucks from…business associates to pay him off."

He shifted guiltily on his knees and Nick translated: "The Mob."

Mario pressed on doggedly, as if he'd been waiting a long time to get it all off his chest. "We buried Rhea's baby and put you in her place. Nobody ever knew the difference."

"But my father…?"

"Andy was in the army, stationed in Germany. He'd never seen the baby. When he came home six weeks after the switch, how could he know?"

"So you expect me to believe that my mother—

that Rhea carried that secret to the grave? How could she do that to me and Daddy?''

Mario looked to be on the verge of tears. "She had to, honey. You were her daughter, the only child she'd ever have. She couldn't lose you, and she didn't want to see her only brother go to jail for the rest of his life for trying to help her. We didn't think you'd ever need to know."

"So what happened?" Cory whispered. "Why *now*?"

Mario licked his lips. "I think Peter's nuts," he said at last, shooting an almost fearful glance at the man shackled to a pillar and muttering to himself beneath his breath. "I mean, *really* nuts. At first his desert rat act was just that—an act to help him disappear and let everyone think he was dead. Now I think he really believes it."

"Then why did you get involved with him again?"

"I didn't think I had a choice. He said if I didn't help him this last time he'd blow the whistle on my part in the original scam. I tried to talk him out of it, but he wouldn't listen. Said he needed money to work the Black Bird Mine, that this time he was going to strike it rich and use every cent to ruin his brother."

"That's why you brought me to Las Vegas? To help a friend?"

"Sweetheart, he hasn't been a friend of mine for a long time. He said he'd go get you himself if I didn't. He promised he wouldn't hurt you, said he just wanted you right under *their* noses. I thought about bumping him off myself, but that's not my line, and what did I care what happened to *them?*" He shot a condemning glance at the Archers, as if this were all their fault. "Pete promised once he got his money, he'd never bother either of us again. When Sammy's watchdog dragged you along to this godforsaken ghost town, I finally woke up."

"Woke up to what?" Her hazel eyes, very like Wil Archer's, now that Nick knew what he knew, widened.

"To the fact that Pete was going to have to kill you all, and by then I knew he was just crazy enough to do it. That's why I came after you, hon—to get you out."

Nick was having trouble restraining himself. "If you weren't Cory's uncle, so help me God, I'd—"

"You're no big hero in all this. Deny it, gumshoe, but *you* knew she was Laura." Mario's eyes turned hard. "You were ready to use her any way you could to save them." He jerked his head toward the Archers.

Cory caught her breath and turned vulnerable eyes on Nick. "Is that true?" she asked, so quietly that only a deathly silence allowed her words to be heard. For the first time since she'd got the news of her parentage, she looked completely conscious of what was going on. "Did you know who I...who I..." She seemed unable to go on.

"Jeez, Cory..." Nick scrambled for the words that would get him off this hook. But he couldn't bring himself to lie to her. Not again. "I suspected," he said at last. "Eventually."

"Eventually. When exactly was eventually?"

"The night Mario drugged us."

Samantha broke in anxiously. "That's when he had your fingerprints matched with my baby's and the real Cory Leblanc's," she blurted. "Now do you believe us?"

"No!" Cory glared at Samantha. "I don't believe Nick would do that and not tell me after what we…" She turned back to Nick, and he must have looked guilty as sin, for all the color fled from her face.

Samantha wouldn't give up. "You know I'm telling the truth. What about the little lightning-shaped mark beneath your left—?"

Wil smacked a hand over her mouth. "Shut up, Sam. Can't you see the girl's in shock?"

And she was. Jumping up, she looked around wildly. "I'm going upstairs. Will you all just leave me alone for a few minutes? I've got to think."

"I'll go with you," Sam said promptly.

"No!" Nick and Wil spoke in unison.

"God, no!" Cory's panicky glance sought Nick. "I trusted you," she said. "All that time you didn't trust me, but I trusted you. How stupid is that?"

"Cory, you've got to let me explain."

"Maybe someday. Not now." Turning, she ran toward the stairs, head down.

Nick groaned. He wanted to go after her, take her in his arms and make her listen—but to what? The answer to that question shocked him: to abject apologies and declarations of undying love. He took a step toward the stairs.

"Hold it, gumshoe." Samantha's tone of command cut through his resolution.

"But I've got to—"

"You've done quite enough for the moment, thank you very much."

"Sam—"

"As you said, give the girl a minute to catch her breath."

"I never said that."

"Then you should have." She slid an arm around his shoulders. "You've done a good job, Nick. I'm in your debt," she said in a husky voice. "But the job's over now, and I'm giving you two weeks—"

"A month," Wil interjected.

"All right, a month's vacation."

"With pay and a bonus."

She grinned. "Yes, Wil, with pay and a *hefty* bonus."

Nick couldn't pull his gaze away from the empty staircase. "Yeah, yeah, there's plenty of time for all that," he muttered, wondering if he'd ever see Cory again. "Right now—"

"Absolutely, right now. As soon as the police finish with you, I want you to take off and not even think about work. One month from today, I'll expect to see you in my office to discuss your next assignment."

Nick felt sick. Was it going to end this way? "Samantha, if you think I'm walking out of here before I have a chance to square things with Cory—"

The heavy front door of the hotel flew open, and suddenly the room was filled with cops. In the ensuing bedlam, Nick never did get a chance to speak to the woman he loved.

ONE MONTH TO THE DAY later, a completely rested but hardly refreshed Nicholas Charles stood looking out Samantha Spade's third-floor office window. The view of the Golden Gate Bridge and San Francisco Bay was as gorgeous as ever, but he couldn't possibly have cared less.

His heart pounded heavily in his chest, as it had since he'd gotten off the airplane from Oklahoma City. His family had spent the last month trying to take his mind off his troubles. All they'd succeeded in doing was convincing him that he'd made the worst mistake of his life when he let Cory get away without a struggle.

But that was the past. Now he knew what he wanted to say to her and he'd say it, whether her witch of a mother approved or not. Samantha could fire him, but she couldn't stop him from telling Cory exactly how he felt about her.

He heard again the sexy cadence of Samantha's spike heels outside the door, as he had heard them the last and only other time he'd been in her office. Holding himself under rigid control, he continued to stare out the window, seeing nothing.

The door opened and he caught a whiff of gardenia, but refused to turn around. The silence stretched out, but he wouldn't break first.

"Well, well," Samantha said in that throaty voice, "if it isn't Nicholas Charles, my number one insurance agent."

"Maybe not number one after you hear what I have to say." *Don't turn around,* he reminded himself. *Keep your cool. Don't let her spook you as she did the last time.*

"Rebellion in the ranks, is it? Speak up, then, and make it snappy."

He heard her close the office door and walk farther into the room, until the carpet muffled her steps.

He sucked in a deep breath. "Sam, I'm in love with your daughter," he said. "If she'll have me, I'm going to marry her, even knowing I'll have to put up with the mother-in-law from hell every day for the rest of my life."

She gasped and made a strangled sound, as if she couldn't form words fast enough to express her outrage.

"Save your breath," he advised. Now that it was out in the open, he felt as if an enormous weight had lifted from his shoulders. "If you get lucky, she may not take me. In that case, I'll have to find a way to change her mind. And I will, if it takes the rest of my life."

"But—"

"Damn it, I love her!" His throat choked up when he said the words, choked up with love, not dread. "She's not only beautiful, she's gutsy and brave and she was meant for *me*, whether she knows it or not. Hell, she was ready to take a bullet for me, so I know she cares."

A curious snuffling sound greeted this pronouncement. *My God*, he thought with horror, *she's crying*. He'd made tough-as-nails S. J. Spade weep like a baby. He turned with a groan. "Don't break down on me. I know you just found her yourself, but..." He stopped speaking to stare.

The woman standing before him wasn't Samantha at all, it was Cory. Or Laura, or whatever they were calling her these days. Hell, he didn't care *who* she was, he loved her.

They met halfway, arms reaching, mouths yearning. When they kissed, he knew everything that mattered: she still cared.

"I love you," he murmured against her lips.

"I love you, too." She rubbed her hands over his shoulders and down his arms. "I needed time. Thank you for letting me have it."

"It almost killed me." He touched her breast through the silky white blouse that might have come from her mother's closet. "Is everything all right now with your new family?"

She began to unbutton his shirt with fingers that trembled. "I accept them, they accept me and we can't be in the same room for five minutes without a fight breaking out."

"I'm sorry." He tugged her blouse away from the waistband of her skirt.

"Don't be. It's done with love. We have a lot to learn about each other, a lot of time to make up for. I give as good as I get, which is something I could never say about my...my first family." He nipped at her earlobe and she caught her breath. "Nick, I'm so glad you're back. Sam said I should make you crawl, but I've missed you too much to play games."

"I missed you, too." Her skirt hit the floor and he stared at long silky legs and licked his lips. "Uhh—before we go any further, is this a good time for me to get down on my hands and knees and apologize for doubting you? Because I will."

"All in due time." She clung to him, her body trembling. "Trust me, Nicky, I'll have you on your hands and knees and every other way I can think of before I'm through with you." She fumbled with his waistband, found the button and popped it open.

"You'll never be through with me." He groaned. "I can hardly wait—" She touched him intimately and his entire body jerked in reaction. "Uhh...do you think we really should—" he rolled his eyes "—right here in your mother's office?"

She dropped her blouse off her shoulders and stood before him in bra, panty hose and high-heeled, ankle-strapped shoes. She smiled a beatific smile. "I made her promise that when she left, she'd lock the door. Is that good enough for you, darling?"

It was, and so was the desk.

Five months later

SAMANTHA WALKED into the bedroom of her San Francisco town house to rouse Wil from a sound sleep. Looking down at him, she felt her heart swell with love and gratitude for the blessings she'd been given—earned, actually. She swallowed hard, thinking that if she wasn't careful she'd be bawling like a baby.

When she touched his shoulder and spoke, her voice didn't sound the least bit sentimental. "Wake up," she demanded. "The wedding is at eleven. Crystal's already gone over to help the bride, so we need to get moving."

Wil opened his eyes and smiled at her. "Good morning to you, too, sweetheart. What time is it?"

"Nine."

"Then there's plenty of time for a little pick-me-up."

"Now, Wil!"

"Now, Sammy!"

He pulled her down on the bed and they wrestled. Eventually, he prevailed, to her delight.

WIL ARCHER WAS INDEED a happy man. Dressing later for the nuptials, he basked in the knowledge that everything had turned out the way it should.

Brother Peter was in a very expensive and highly regarded funny farm, weaving baskets and explaining how he was going to use his brother's daughter to extort money to reopen the Black Bird Mine; Mark-Mario was on probation and working at a halfway house in Las Vegas; Samantha was Wil's wife once more, which she'd always been in his heart; and their long-lost daughter, Laura, now an employee of her mother's "insurance" agency, was about to become the bride of Sammy's number one operative.

Wil expressed his satisfaction to his own bride as she applied red lipstick before her dressing table mirror.

The golden tube poised before her mouth, Samantha's sudden smile radiated joy. "Once they're married, do you realize who they'll be?" she demanded.

He shrugged. "Nick and Laura Charles."

Sammy, his normally self-possessed wife, collapsed in helpless laughter. "Darling," she said when she could speak again, "you've just *got* to start reading Dashiell Hammett!"

HARLEQUIN®

Temptation®

It's hotter than a winter fire.
It's a BLAZE!

In January 1999 stay warm with another
one of our bold, provocative, *ultra-sexy*
Temptation novels.

#715 TANTALIZING
by Lori Foster

It was lust at first sight—but Josie and Mark were both
pretending to be other people! They were giving new
meaning to the term "blind date." How to unravel the web
of deceit? And still hang on to that sexy stranger...

BLAZE!
Red-hot reads from Temptation!

Available wherever Harlequin books are sold.

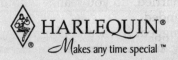

HARLEQUIN®
Makes any time special ™

Take 2 bestselling love stories FREE

Plus get a FREE surprise gift!

Special Limited-Time Offer

Mail to Harlequin Reader Service®

> 3010 Walden Avenue
> P.O. Box 1867
> Buffalo, N.Y. 14240-1867

YES! Please send me 2 free Harlequin Temptation® novels and my free surprise gift. Then send me 4 brand-new novels every month, which I will receive before they appear in bookstores. Bill me at the low price of $3.12 each plus 25¢ delivery and applicable sales tax, if any.* That's the complete price, and a saving of over 10% off the cover prices—quite a bargain! I understand that accepting the books and gift places me under no obligation ever to buy any books. I can always return a shipment and cancel at any time. Even if I never buy another book from Harlequin, the 2 free books and the surprise gift are mine to keep forever.

142 HEN CH7G

Name	(PLEASE PRINT)	
Address	Apt. No.	
City	State	Zip

This offer is limited to one order per household and not valid to present Harlequin Temptation® subscribers. *Terms and prices are subject to change without notice. Sales tax applicable in N.Y.

UTEMP-98   ©1990 Harlequin Enterprises Limited

For a limited time, Harlequin and Silhouette have an offer you just can't refuse.

In November and December 1998:

BUY **ANY** TWO HARLEQUIN
OR SILHOUETTE BOOKS and
SAVE $10.00
off future purchases

OR BUY ANY THREE HARLEQUIN OR SILHOUETTE BOOKS
AND **SAVE $20.00** OFF FUTURE PURCHASES!

(each coupon is good for $1.00 off the purchase of two
Harlequin or Silhouette books)

JUST BUY 2 HARLEQUIN OR SILHOUETTE BOOKS, SEND US YOUR
NAME, ADDRESS AND 2 PROOFS OF PURCHASE (CASH REGISTER
RECEIPTS) AND HARLEQUIN WILL SEND YOU A COUPON BOOKLET
WORTH $10.00 OFF FUTURE PURCHASES OF HARLEQUIN OR
SILHOUETTE BOOKS IN 1999. SEND US 3 PROOFS OF PURCHASE AND
WE WILL SEND YOU 2 COUPON BOOKLETS WITH A TOTAL SAVING OF
$20.00. (ALLOW 4-6 WEEKS DELIVERY) OFFER EXPIRES
DECEMBER 31, 1998.

I accept your offer! Please send me a coupon booklet(s), to:

NAME: _____

ADDRESS: _____

CITY: _____ STATE/PROV.: _____ POSTAL/ZIP CODE: _____

Send your name and address, along with your cash register
receipts for proofs of purchase, to:

In the U.S.	In Canada
Harlequin Books	**Harlequin Books**
P.O. Box 9057	**P.O. Box 622**
Buffalo, NY	**Fort Erie, Ontario**
14269	**L2A 5X3**

PHQ4982

HARLEQUIN®

Temptation®

He's strong. He's sexy.
He's up for grabs!

Harlequin Temptation and
Texas Men magazine present:

1998 Mail Order Men

#691 THE LONE WOLF
by Sandy Steen—July 1998

#695 SINGLE IN THE SADDLE
by Vicki Lewis Thompson—August 1998

#699 SINGLE SHERIFF SEEKS...
by Jo Leigh—September 1998

#703 STILL HITCHED, COWBOY
by Leandra Logan—October 1998

#707 TALL, DARK AND RECKLESS
by Lyn Ellis—November 1998

#711 MR. DECEMBER
by Heather MacAllister—December 1998

Mail Order Men—
Satisfaction Guaranteed!

Available wherever Harlequin books are sold.

HARLEQUIN®
Makes any time special ™

Look us up on-line at: http://www.romance.net   HTEMOM